Down Garrapata Road

Down Garrapata Road

by

Anne Estevis

 HAMPTON-BROWN

Hampton-Brown
P.O. Box 223220
Carmel, California 93922
800-333-3510
www.hampton-brown.com

Printed in the United States of America

ISBN 13: 987-0-7362-3197-8
ISBN 10: 0-7362-3197-8

06 07 08 09 10 11 12 13 14 15 10 9 8 7 6 5 4 3 2 1

This collection is dedicated to María de Jesús Estevis, a dear sister-in-law and a source of much of the inspiration that led me to create the stories of Garrapata Road.

Contents

Introduction

Down Garrapata Road is a collection of stories by Anne Estevis. The setting is rural Texas during the 1940s and 1950s. Four Mexican American families, the Chávezes, the Bermúdezes, the Zambranos, and the Palomas, all live on Garrapata Road. Although each story focuses on only one of the families, characters from all the families appear throughout the book. Telling the stories in this intertwined way, Estevis shows how these families form a close community. The stories are told from the **perspective** of one young member of each of the four families. They tell of the **expectations** placed on them by their families and the community. The stories also tell how the expectations change as family obligations, the community, and even the world change.

In the 1940s and 1950s Mexican culture dominated the Texas region where this book takes place. The stores sold products from Mexico. The restaurants served Mexican food. Most people spoke Spanish. Yet these immigrants knew that they had to learn English in order to succeed in the United States. During this time, many Mexican Americans faced discrimination and other injustices. New immigrants often came to the United States

Key Concepts

perspective *n.* view, outlook

expectation *n.* hope or wish; something that is supposed to happen

9

as farm workers. Their low-paying jobs caused them to live in poverty.

Both poverty and the language barrier kept many Mexican Americans from attending school regularly. Texas had a mandatory school attendance law during the 1930s and 1940s. But the state did not enforce it. Families kept children home to help them in the fields. Other children were too frightened to go to school because they did not speak English.

Serving in the military during World War II was one way for young Mexican American men to get an education and escape poverty. Soldiers that came home from the war were often given educations and other basic benefits. Many young American men were drafted to fight in the war against their will. In contrast, the young inhabitants of Garrapata Road eagerly volunteer to go to war.

This collection of stories shows a **generation** of young Mexican Americans who are growing up during a time of worldwide change and conflict. Their lives must bridge two cultures. They struggle to fit in both their traditional Mexican culture and the modern American culture. The stories that take place before World War II show an **innocence** and excitement about life. They are about first love, fancy dresses, and parties for young men going off to war. The stories that take

Key Concepts

generation *n.* group of people born and living around the same time

innocence *n.* lack of knowledge or understanding

place during and after World War II show a dramatic change in attitude and **maturity**. Characters face the consequences of their friends and family members dying in combat or being captured by the enemy as prisoners of war. These later stories deal with the harsh realities of growing up and moving away from home. Estevis invites readers to experience the good and the bad, the fun and the seriousness, of life on Garrapata Road.

▶ **The Families of Garrapata**

The Chávez Family	The Bermúdez Family
Carmen (grandmother)	Abuela (grandmother)
Anselmo (Papá)	don Tacho (Papá)
Chencha (Mamá)	Persíngula (Mamá)
Aunt Eloína, or Tía Pina (aunt)	Benito, or Benny (son)
Telésfora, or Chatita (daughter)	Zulema (daughter)
Chuy (son)	Paco, or Francisco (son)
Keno (son)	Agustín (son)
	Pancracio (son)
The Zambrano Family	**The Paloma Family**
Grandmother	don Nicho (Papá)
Papá	Mamá
Mamá	Juana (daughter)
Víctor (son)	Nilda (daughter)
Mariano (son)	Pedro, or Pete (son)
Teódulo, or Teddy (son)	Roberto (son)
Cookie (cousin)	Zeke (son) and Rita (Zeke's wife)
	Tío Ramón (uncle)

Key Concepts

maturity *n.* being mentally developed or grown up

I

The Chávez Family

Tía Pina and the *Chupasangre*

In the summer when I was eleven years old, my aunt Eloína came to Texas to visit us. She showed up at our place unexpectedly. All she had with her was a rumpled paper bag containing her few possessions. Tía Pina, as my brothers and I called Eloína, was my father's oldest sister. She had stayed in Mexico when my father and his brothers had come to the Lower Rio Grande Valley many years before. Tía Pina had never married. Now, **having outlived all of her kinfolk in Mexico**, and finding herself **destitute**, she had come to my father for help.

Mamá told Papá with **a disgruntled** tone to her voice, "Anselmo, didn't I always tell you we would eventually have to take care of Eloína?"

"Chencha, please. My poor sister has no one else to turn to," my father meekly replied. He was sharpening his knife and

....

having outlived all of her kinfolk in Mexico her family in Mexico was dead

destitute poor; without any money

a disgruntled an unhappy; an angry

didn't look up.

"Well, I knew she'd never marry. I always told you she was too ugly to catch a husband!" Mamá said.

"Hush, Chencha. Our daughter is listening to you," my father said as he looked up at me where I stood by the kitchen table.

Poor Tía Pina. She really wasn't pretty with her short, frizzy, gray and brown hair that seemed to jump right out from her head. Her body was skinny and her muscular legs would have looked better on a man. **Smallpox** had left scars on her face and she had a patch of black fuzz growing below her nose. I thought she was wonderful. I didn't mind sharing my little lean-to room with her because she was pleasant and treated me with kindness. In fact, she brought **a breath of fresh air** into my life.

"Anselmo, I don't want to be a burden to you and Chencha," Tía Pina had announced the day she arrived. "I want to **make my own way**. Is there any work here for me?"

My father shook his head and said, "There's no paid work except seasonal fieldwork and I already have a hired man."

So Tía Pina attempted to help Mamá with chores around the house. Mamá didn't seem very pleased with Tía Pina's efforts.

"Your sister **has the grace of an ox**!" my mother complained to my father. "She throws water all over the kitchen when she

....

Smallpox A childhood disease
a breath of fresh air new excitement
make my own way work and make money
has the grace of an ox is very clumsy

washes dishes. She breaks what she can and puts things where I can't find them. And, she can't cook at all!" Mamá stood with her hands on her hips, scowling at my father.

"Eloína is just trying to help. She doesn't want to be a burden to anyone," Papá said as he wiped the perspiration from his face and sighed.

"Well, I suggest you find her something to do outside the house where she can't do any more damage to my things!" Mamá replied.

That's when Papá came up with a brilliant idea. It was vegetable picking time and he knew that the **itinerant** field workers on the neighboring farms had no place to buy cold soda pop or other items of refreshment. So, under the Chinese tallow tree in our backyard, Papá set up a table on which Tía Pina laid out a variety of sweet bread that Papá had brought from a bakery in town. Bottles of RC Cola and Delaware Punch were put into a washtub with a block of ice and then covered with a piece of old canvas. Tía Pina was now **in business** and Papá didn't waste time telling the field workers from the farms up and down Garrapata Road where they could get refreshments.

Many workers came to our yard during their lunch breaks to buy Tía Pina's drinks and sweet bread. Some even came in the

....

itinerant traveling, migrant
in business ready to open the refreshment stand

late afternoon to have a cold drink or just to rest under our tallow tree. Tía Pina was friendly to her customers and her business **thrived**. It was apparent that she was well liked by the workers, especially by one named Agapito. He was a short, stocky man with a huge black mustache. At noon he was the first to arrive and the last to leave. He usually drank three RC Colas as he rested in the shade of the tree, patted our dogs, and talked with Tía Pina. Most evenings after work, Agapito would return to the field workers' quarters to bathe, change clothes, and grab his guitar. Then he would come to our yard to drink a few RC Colas and visit with Tía Pina. He would play and sing beautiful songs for Tía Pina and me, and sometimes Tía Pina would sing along with him. Most of the time, however, he and my aunt just talked about their lives in Mexico.

Mamá must have **taken special notice of** Agapito because she said to Papá, "Anselmo, does don Tacho know that one of his field workers likes to **loiter** in our backyard with your sister?"

"I doubt it. What difference does it make to you?" My father stood and looked squarely at my mother. "Don Tacho pays the workers by the amount they pick. If they don't work, they don't get paid."

"Well, I'm warning you. **No good will come from this**,"

....

thrived was very successful
taken special notice of seen what was happening with
loiter waste time; stay
No good will come from this He is trouble

Mamá replied as she made a fist and punched the dough she was preparing for tortillas.

Tía Pina sold her drinks and sweet bread for most of the summer, faithfully putting her profits away in little Bull Durham tobacco bags that the workers gave her when they emptied them. She hid the little bags under her pillow, where she said she was sure her money was safe.

As the crops were picked and the field workers moved on, it became evident that Tía Pina would have to **discontinue her business venture**. This seemed to **dishearten** her, and she became somewhat quiet and withdrawn. That is, until a strange thing happened one night.

It was a hot humid night and Tía Pina and I had moved our mattress over against the wall under the open window. Tía Pina slept next to the window because I was afraid of the geckos that ran around on the outside of the window screen. Sometime that night something awakened me. I'm not sure what it was. Perhaps it had been a noise, but I recall that the bedsheet covering my body seemed to move. I turned toward Tía Pina and saw her sitting up on the mattress, facing the window. It was too dark to see anything distinctly, but I thought I saw someone standing on the outside with the upper part of the body coming through the

....

discontinue her business venture stop selling drinks
dishearten sadden

window. Whoever it was seemed to be holding on to Tía Pina and biting her neck. I screamed. Tía Pina screamed. Then I saw the window screen fall back into place.

Next I heard my mother's bare feet running across the kitchen floor as she yelled, "I'm coming, Chatita! I'm coming!"

Papá was not far behind her. He had taken only a few seconds to light the lantern. My brothers, who slept in a one-room sleeping house in the yard, came up to the window and looked into the room.

"What's wrong?" my brother Chuy asked. "I heard someone screaming."

Tía Pina didn't seem to be able to talk. I quickly explained to my startled family what I thought I had seen.

"That's strange. We didn't hear anything or see anything," said Chuy.

"And why didn't the dogs bark?" asked my brother Keno. "If a stranger had been out here, those dogs would have **raised hell**."

"But I really think I saw someone biting Tía Pina's neck," I said **in dismay**.

Papá moved the lantern closer to my aunt. There was a rather large red mark on her neck. She quickly put her hand over the mark.

....

raised hell barked loudly to let us know
in dismay fearfully

"My God! What's wrong with your neck, Eloína?" Papá asked. "Move your hand so I can **get a better look**."

Tía Pina reluctantly took her hand away.

"*¡Ay, Dios!* He did get her on the neck!" Mamá said.

"It must have been the *Chupasangre*," my brother Keno said with a serious tone.

"*Chupasangre?* Bloodsucker?" I asked. "You mean like a vampire?" I moved closer to Mamá.

"Yes. That's what I mean," answered Keno.

"How did he get the screen open?" Mamá asked.

Chuy inspected the screen. "There's no cut in the screen. Someone had to have **unlatched** it from inside the room," he said.

We all looked at Tía Pina.

"Maybe I left it unlatched the last time I cleaned the sill," Tía Pina said quickly. "Yes. I'm sure that's what I must have done."

The story of the *Chupasangre* traveled up and down Garrapata Road. All of my friends came by our house wanting to see my aunt's neck. The red mark stayed on her neck for about ten days. Some of the stupid neighborhood boys would drive by

---

get a better look see it clearly
¡Ay, Dios! Oh, my goodness! (in Spanish)
unlatched opened, unlocked

our house at night honking their horns and yelling, "Here comes the *Chupasangre!*"

After the night Tía Pina's neck was molested, I didn't want to sleep with the mattress next to the window. Tía Pina didn't seem as afraid as I was, but of course she was a grown woman. She said we would **die of heat stroke** if we didn't sleep where we could get some air, so we left the mattress next to the window. Every night I expected the *Chupasangre* to return and make me his next victim, so I wrapped my extra dress around my neck as tight as I could **stand it**. But the *Chupasangre* was keeping itself busy elsewhere. We heard that he frightened don Tacho Bermúdez's eighty-year-old mother when she went out to the **privy** one night. In fact, almost every unmarried woman over the age of eighteen in our neighborhood reported seeing or being bothered by the *Chupasangre*. Many of them did indeed have red marks on their necks, and they gladly showed their "injuries" to any interested onlooker.

Mamá was not pleased with these reports or with Tía Pina. "See what your sister has caused, Anselmo. This is a disgrace! *¡Ay, Dios, mío!* What will our neighbors think?"

"Why do you say Eloína caused all of this?" Papá asked.

"Because she did! I know she did. Oh, this is a terrible

....

die of heat stroke get sick from being too hot
stand it without being uncomfortable
privy outdoor bathroom

scandal! I wish she were gone from this house!"

"Please, Chencha. Be quiet. She'll hear you," Papá replied. "Besides, I don't think anything more will happen."

But it did happen. The *Chupasangre* returned to our house several weeks later. It was a moonlit night. I awakened just in time to see him pulling Tía Pina out of the window. I couldn't believe what I was witnessing. My aunt didn't protest at all! In fact, she never said a word. I should have screamed, but I didn't. Perhaps it was because there was something vaguely familiar about the *Chupasangre*. I felt somewhat **beguiled** as I leaned against the windowsill and watched as Tía Pina and the *Chupasangre* walked away holding hands. Besides taking Tía Pina, the *Chupasangre* must have taken her money, because when I checked under her pillow, the little tobacco bags were gone. In the moonlight I could see that Tía Pina carried her old crumpled paper bag and the *Chupasangre* had what looked suspiciously like a guitar hanging from his shoulder.

....

scandal embarrassment; incident that will hurt our reputation

beguiled tricked, betrayed

BEFORE YOU MOVE ON...

1. **Narrator** Reread pages 20–22. Who is telling this story? How do you know?

2. **Conclusions** Reread pages 20–23. Who is the *Chupasangre* and why is Tía Pina not scared of him?

The Dancing Queens of Garrapata Road

My childhood was spent on our farm on Garrapata Road in South Texas. I never thought there was anything wrong with living on a road named for a small **blood-sucking arachnid** until I heard my brother Keno **admonishing** my oldest brother Chuy for referring to our road as Garrapata.

"Hey! Stop saying Garrapata Road. It's Garland Potter Road!"

Chuy laughed and responded, "So what's wrong with living on Tick Road? It's better than Cockroach Street or Bedbug Avenue."

"It's just not Garrapata. That's what's wrong," Keno replied.

"Garrapata is **a nickname**. Right, Chatita?" Chuy turned to me and gently touched the end of my nose with the tip of his index finger. "*Your* nickname is Chatita. I've even forgotten your real name." He began to laugh.

....

blood-sucking arachnid insect
admonishing yelling at; getting upset with
a nickname just a funny name

"I don't see anything wrong with saying Garrapata Road," I responded.

Keno pointed his finger at me and said, "Look, little sister, just keep saying Garrapata and see how **you'll be made fun of** at school. The *americanos* will really laugh at you."

I didn't care about school right then. It was summer. All I was concerned about was what I was going to wear to the party we would be going to that night. I was tired of wearing the same old **hand-me-down** dress over and over again. Just once I wanted to know what it felt like to wear a fancy new dress bought especially for me. But my mother said that a store-bought dress was just too expensive, that we could not afford to use our money on such things.

Getting a new dress **weighed heavy on my mind** because of the invitation given us by our neighbor don Tacho Bermúdez. He had come by our house earlier that morning in his big farm truck. I would have stayed asleep longer, but don Tacho's truck made very loud noises. He and my father sat in the *cocina* drinking coffee and talking about what would happen now that the United States was in the war. I decided to stay on my little *colchón* in the lean-to just off the kitchen to listen to their conversation.

....

you'll be made fun of you will be teased
hand-me-down used; previously owned
weighed heavy on my mind was a big concern
colchón mattress (in Spanish)

"I tell you, Tacho, I don't want Chuy going into the military. I need him here on the farm, but he wants to go off and kill some Germans," my father had lamented over his coffee, which he always sweetened with four or five spoonfuls of sugar. "He can't go. He's only sixteen, just a boy!"

"*¡Ay!* I feel the same about my sons. And now, the two oldest ones have already signed up and will be leaving soon," our neighbor replied.

I didn't understand why the boys from Garrapata Road wanted to go to a foreign country and **make war against** the Germans. The boys had been talking a lot about that terrible man Hitler. I knew that the Japanese had bombed American ships at a place called Pearl Harbor. But these events **had little relevance to** me. At fourteen, my world was here on my father's twenty-acre farm, and up and down the dusty dirt road that I called Garrapata Road.

My father and don Tacho continued talking and drinking coffee. They talked about their crops and about the weather and about how don Pancho was going blind from the *carnocidad* that was growing in the corners of his eyes.

I had almost fallen back to sleep when I heard don Tacho say, "I'm inviting you and your **esteemed family to a fiesta** at my

---

make war against fight
had little relevance to did not really affect
esteemed family to a fiesta respected family to a party

ranch tonight. My boys soon will be leaving for the Army and I want to give them a farewell party."

When I heard we were invited to a fiesta, I could hardly keep from laughing aloud, except I didn't dare because then I would be in trouble with my father. Perhaps I should not seem too excited about going to the party because someone might suspect that I liked Benny Bermúdez, one of don Tacho's sons. Benny's sister Zulema had told me that Benny liked me. Well, he *should* like me. I always saved him a seat on the school bus because the good seats were all taken by the time we got to the Bermúdez farm at the far end of Garrapata Road. Benny didn't always accept my offer, and when he did we usually rode along in silence. Maybe he would talk to me tonight at the party.

I spent most of the morning doing my regular Saturday chores. When I was done I washed and ironed my brown gingham dress for the party. It was becoming **tattered**, but it looked better than my only other dress, a blue batiste that I usually slept in. As for shoes, all I could do was clean my only pair. They were brown oxfords that had taken on a fuzzy gray look from wear. They were **handed down** to me from my ugly cousin, Eufemia. The shoes had the outline of her feet permanently formed in them. The **humps from her bunions**

....

tattered old and torn; ragged
handed down given
humps from her bunions lumps on her feet

made the shoes look out of shape. Every time I looked down at my feet in those ugly shoes, I remembered how much I disliked my cousin. But they were my party shoes for as long as I could fit in them.

On the way to the party that night, I was allowed to ride in the **cab** of my father's pickup truck so I wouldn't get dusty. Keno and I, being the younger ones, usually rode in the bed of the truck. This time, however, my mother told Chuy to **trade places with me**. He didn't protest, but I could tell from the face that he made that he didn't like it. He probably thought that because he was oldest he should ride up in the cab with my parents. I've always noticed that oldest brothers have the idea that they are **second in command** of the family and that younger brothers and sisters should **pay them homage**. Well, this time, I arrived looking fresh and clean even though I was wearing my old brown dress and ill-fitting shoes.

The fiesta at the Bermúdez farm was like most of the celebrations held at the farms in South Texas. Earlier in the day don Tacho's boys had cleared and cleaned the barren yard

....

cab front
trade places with me sit in back instead of me
second in command leaders
pay them homage respect them

and sprinkled it down with water to settle the dirt. Benches had been assembled from fruit crates with wide planks placed from crate to crate. In the center of the large oval area formed by the arrangement of the benches, a pole was **erected** and two kerosene lanterns were hung on a crossbar near the top.

The musicians, with accordions and guitars, were already playing by the time we sat down on some benches in the patio. That was only after I and my entire family **made the rounds**, greeting and shaking hands of all the people who were gathered there. Then I saw Benny Bermúdez standing outside the oval area talking to some of his friends. He looked straight at me and then quickly looked away. I noticed how handsome he appeared in a starched shirt and a new pair of khaki trousers. He had combed his wavy black hair **into a pompadour that looked** as if it had been drenched with La Parrot brilliantine.

My parents got up and started dancing to the lively music, as did dozens of couples. Even the young children were dancing around in the yard, and some of the adolescent girls danced with one another. I didn't want to dance because I felt rather ugly in my old dress and deformed shoes. I sat off to the side and out of the glare of the lanterns. The patio got crowded with people who arrived in farm trucks and in *guallines* pulled by horses and

....

erected built

made the rounds walked around and talked to everyone

into a pompadour that looked so that the front of it was sticking straight up

mules. Moments later, Lupe Mondragón and Regina Roybal arrived and came to sit with me. They both lived on farms near us and we saw one another often. Of all the girls from Garrapata Road, I liked them best.

I was talking and laughing with my two friends when Benny Bermúdez's sister, Zulema, beckoned for me to come over to her.

"Benito wants you to meet him over there under the big fresno tree," she said as she indicated the direction of the tree with a toss of her head.

I was **elated**. "When?" I asked.

"Now, *tonta*," she whispered in a raspy voice.

I chose to ignore what she had just called me simply because I was overjoyed. My heart seemed to flutter around in my chest and **my breathing was a little labored**. I quickly moved out of the reach of the lantern light and hurried to the large tree at the side of don Tacho's tractor shed.

I stood alone under the tree for several minutes peering into the night, hoping to see Benny Bermúdez hurrying toward me. But when I finally saw him coming over, he didn't hurry. Instead, he slowly sauntered up to within a few feet of me, his hands in his pockets.

"Watta ya want, girl?" he blurted out.

....

elated excited, thrilled

tonta stupid (in Spanish)

my breathing was a little labored I had a hard time breathing

It seemed to me that he wasn't too excited about our **romantic rendezvous**.

"What do you mean, what do *I* want?" I retorted. "Didn't you tell your sister to have me meet you here?" I was beginning to feel disheartened. Something was **amiss**.

"*No, **muchacha estúpida**. My sister said *you* wanted to talk to me. Why should I want to talk to you?"

Before I could respond, I heard a faint plopping sound. Benny quickly took one of his hands out of his pocket and ran it over the top of his head. A distinct odor of chicken excrement **permeated** the air and a rustling up in the tree hinted at its source.

Benny leaned over and attempted to knock the stuff from his hair but it got all over his nice starched shirt and his new khaki trousers. The odor intensified. Then Benny whirled around and ran off into the night, spitting and gagging and making *gargajos*. It was at that moment that I knew my love for Benito Bermúdez was not to be.

The rest of the night would have been boring and uneventful for me if it hadn't been for Juana and Nilda, the Paloma sisters. My friends and I thought they were rich because they owned three pairs of shoes between them, and because their mother didn't have to make their dresses and underwear. Their father

....

romantic rendezvous private meeting
amiss wrong
muchacha estúpida stupid girl (in Spanish)
permeated filled

always bought all their clothing at the mercantile. Secretly, I envied those Paloma sisters. I even hated them a little when they arrived at the party in the most beautiful dancing frocks I had ever seen. Juana wore a blue one made of a soft shiny fabric. It came to her ankles and had ruffles over the shoulders. It was cut somewhat low in the back. Nilda's dress was almost identical, except it was pink. Both frocks were festooned with lace of a kind that I had never seen. What really impressed me were the sisters' satin slippers that matched the color of their dresses. The slippers had little high heels and were embellished on the toes with satin **rosettes. My avarice knew no bounds. I coveted** one of those dancing dresses!

Females of all ages swarmed around the Paloma sisters after they made their grand entrance into the patio. There were "oohs" and "aahs" coming from every direction. All the girls wanted to touch the delicate shiny fabric of the dresses and run the lace between their fingers.

Lupe Mondragón asked the first question: "Where did you get these beautiful dresses?"

Juana, the older Paloma sister, answered, "Our father went to San Antonio last week to sell his leftover tomatoes. He bought our dresses there in a very fancy ladies' store."

....

rosettes ribbons shaped like roses

My avarice knew no bounds. I felt uncontrollably jealous and greedy.

coveted really wanted

The second, but most important question was asked by Lulu Larralde: "How much did they cost?"

Juana answered again. "They were very expensive. Four dollars each."

Someone asked about the slippers.

"They're an extra two dollars," responded Nilda before Juana could answer.

Quickly I **did a mental computation**. Six dollars! I had never had six dollars all at one time in my life! Then I heard Juana say something that made me feel **tingly all over**.

"My father is returning to San Antonio next week. If any of you want him to bring you a dress and slippers, just give me the money."

Without delay, everybody rushed to their own parents to **try their luck**. In less than half an hour some of the girls began handing six dollars to the Paloma sisters to give to their father.

"I want a green dancing dress," said Hermenegilda Segovia.

"Please ask your father to bring me a beautiful yellow frock," said Tencha Tovar.

"I'd really like a red one if they have it. Otherwise, I want a dusty rose or even a sky blue," reported Simona de los Santos.

And so it went on for a good part of the night that money

....

did a mental computation added the amounts
tingly all over excited, hopeful
try their luck see if they would buy them a dress

and orders for dancing frocks were given to the Paloma sisters. I wanted to ask my father if he would give don Nicho Paloma six dollars to buy me a splendid dancing dress and a pair of the little satin slippers. But I didn't think it was a good idea to ask Papá at the party. So, on the way home that night, while sitting between my parents, I asked my father if he would let me buy one of those dresses. I tried not to breathe while I waited for the response that he was quick in delivering.

"No."

His answer was what I already expected. Nevertheless, I was disappointed, but I knew better than to question my father's decision. I would never directly **probe his judgment or demand a rationale from him**; instead I would approach my mother.

The next day I found my mother sitting outside the house plucking the feathers from a **pullet** she had just killed. I had just finished my morning chores, so I sat down near her to rest a few minutes.

"Mamá, I want a dancing dress like the Paloma sisters have. Why won't Papá buy me one?"

My mother dropped the chicken back down into the bucket of hot water, wiped her sweaty face with her apron, and said, "He doesn't like those dresses. He says they are too fancy."

....

probe his judgment or demand a rationale from him ask him why he decided not to buy me the dress

pullet young chicken

She went back to plucking the chicken and I went into the house. My brother Chuy was alone at the kitchen table drinking coffee and eating a piece of *pan dulce*. He had overheard my conversation with Mamá.

"I'm sorry you can't get a dress," Chuy said.

"I really want a fancy dress to wear to the fiestas," I responded. "I think there will be more good-bye parties with so many of the boys going into the Army."

"Yes, I know. All of my friends are going. Papá says I'm too young to **enlist**, but I want to go anyway."

That night Chuy went off with his friends and didn't come home for two days. He had gone to San Antonio to attempt to join the Army. He thought he could lie about his age in San Antonio where no one knew him, but his plan did not work. I did not know if I was happy or sad for him. But I was delighted when Chuy handed me a large paper bag. In it was a beautiful lilac-colored dancing dress, more splendid than the dresses of the Paloma sisters. Mine was made of a double layer of shimmering soft knit jersey with purple satin ribbon inserts running the length of the dress all the way around.

There were deep ruffles around the neck, as well as around the bottom of the skirt. Chuy had even remembered the

....

pan dulce cake, pastry (in Spanish)
enlist join; sign up

matching lilac-colored slippers. Mine didn't have satin rosettes like those of the Paloma sisters. Mine had fluffy balls of purple rabbit fur.

What a wonderful gift from my brother! After checking to make sure I was alone, I put on my new dress and my new slippers. It was a little difficult to dance around because I was not **accustomed to** shoes with high heels, but I knew I could overcome this slight problem by practicing a little bit every day. I could hardly wait until the next fiesta so I could wear the most beautiful dress I was sure I would ever own.

I didn't have to wait very long. Two weeks after Chuy bought me the dress, we were invited to a fiesta at don Tavo Guzmán's farm. It was a **marvelous** party and I remember it well. In the yellow glare of the kerosene lanterns, on the packed earth of Guzmán's patio, Lupe Mondragón, Regina Roybal, and I, along with **a half dozen** other girls dressed in new pastel frocks, danced, and danced, and danced. That night, each of us pranced like a queen in our very own nightgown and matching satin bedroom slippers.

....

accustomed to used to
marvelous wonderful
a half dozen six

The Whistle

My **paternal grandmother** Carmen was a tiny woman, not even five feet tall. She came to live with us because she said she needed to help my mother with the **heavy load** of raising a family. Having my grandmother around was usually pleasant, however I remember a time when I wished she would find another family to care for. It was during the late autumn when I was fourteen years old. My parents had gone to San Antonio because my mother's father was very ill.

Before leaving, Mamá said to my **abuela**, "Please take care of Chatita and the boys while I am gone."

Then Mamá turned around and quietly said to my brothers and me, "Children, please take care of your grandmother."

For several days we all took good care of one another. Then, on Saturday, the third day of my parents' absence, **a cool front blew in** a short while after we had eaten our noon meal. It wasn't

....

paternal grandmother father's mother
heavy load hard work; responsibility
abuela grandmother (in Spanish)
a cool front blew in it started to get cold outside

terribly cold, just a little nippy.

My grandmother took note of the pleasant weather and remarked, "What a nice day it is! I think I will clean the storage shed." She retied her sagging apron, put on her sweater, and marched directly out to the shed.

While my grandmother **toiled** in the shed, I went about my Saturday chores as usual: washing the bedding, cleaning out the ice box, feeding the chickens, cleaning the lantern chimneys, and polishing my only pair of shoes. My brothers Keno and Chuy had been instructed by our father to prepare the fields for winter vegetable planting, so I was alone in the house. I liked it this way because I could do my work without interruption and get finished sooner.

In the late afternoon I took some vegetable peelings out to the chickens and noticed that the sky was cloudy and the wind was blowing harder than it had earlier. The day was turning cold. I glanced toward the storage shed and wondered how much longer my abuela would be working. I faintly heard what sounded like a goat **bleating**, so I looked around. Seeing nothing, I hurried back into the house to finish my chores. I especially wanted to get the lanterns put back together before dark.

Later I went out to get some firewood and while picking

....

toiled worked
bleating crying

up small pieces of kindling from near the woodpile I heard again what I thought was a bleating goat. Still, I couldn't see the animal. Perhaps Keno or Chuy had brought home a **kid** to slaughter. They did that occasionally. We all enjoyed the savory meat of *cabrito*; I was beginning to feel hungry just thinking about it. I thought I should look for the animal, but decided to get the fire in the stove going first because I could see Chuy coming toward the house on the tractor. Keno was already at the tractor shed, and the boys usually wanted coffee as soon as they got to the house.

The house quickly warmed from the fire in the cookstove. I was just putting on the pot for coffee when my brothers stomped into the kitchen.

"It's really getting cold out there!" said Chuy as he hovered over the big stove.

"Is the coffee ready, Chatita?" Keno asked.

I shook my head. "What about the goat? Are you going to **butcher it**?"

Neither answered. Chuy stopped warming his hands and turned away from the stove to look at me. Keno continued washing up in the enamel wash pan.

"I said, are you going to butcher the goat?"

....

kid young goat
butcher it kill it so we can eat it

"What goat are you talking about?" responded Keno.

"We don't have any goats," said Chuy.

I gasped and said, "Oh, my goodness! Come with me! Hurry!" I bounded out the kitchen door with my brothers behind me.

As we approached the storage shed I could see that the outside latch hook on the door was in place. I flipped the hook tip and flung open the door. There, sitting on the floor, wrapped up **in burlap bags like a mummy**, was a cold and shivering grandmother. She tried to talk, but her voice was almost gone.

My brothers helped the tiny woman to her feet and Keno carried her into the house as quickly as he could. All the way she was croaking like a frog, but I'm sure I discerned the words *"¡Huercos desgraciados!"* repeated over and over. This meant that we were wretched brats, or maybe worse.

My brothers placed her in the chair nearest the kitchen stove while I fetched a soft woolen blanket to wrap her in. Chuy poured a cup of coffee and set it before her. Then we all sat down around the table staring at our obviously **infuriated** grandmother.

"What unfortunate children you are. You **have no brains**!" she said in a raspy voice. Her entire body was shivering. "You left me to die out there!" She shook her fist at each one of us and

....

in burlap bags like a mummy tight in cloth bags to keep her warm

infuriated very angry

have no brains are not smart

then looked squarely at me. "You, Telésfora. You must be deaf." She shook a crooked index finger at me.

I knew she was very angry with me because she used my real name.

"I called and called for you. The wind blew the door shut and it locked. All afternoon I yelled, but you didn't come. I nearly **froze to death**!" She scowled and slowly turned her head away from me.

"But, I didn't hear you," I answered. "I'm sorry. Please, Abuelita. I'm truly sorry!"

How could I have confused my grandmother's voice with that of a bleating goat? I felt terribly guilty and ashamed. I knew that the shed door was **prone** to latch by itself if it was slammed. That's why a wooden stake for propping the door open was usually kept nearby. But this time the stake had not been used, and now my grandmother was shaking and shivering and glaring at me.

"Just you wait, Telésfora. Just you wait until your father gets home. I'll have him punish you," she said and her bottom lip quivered and her nostrils flared.

....

froze to death died because it was so cold in there
prone likely

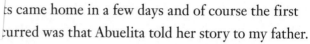

ts came home in a few days and of course the first
thing occurred was that Abuelita told her story to my father.

"Son, Telésfora left me locked in the storage shed all
afternoon on Saturday. I called and called for her, but she
declares she didn't hear me. She says she heard a goat bleating.
Can you imagine that I could possibly sound like a goat?" my
grandmother said.

My father was very concerned, of course. I admitted to
him that, indeed, I had mistakenly thought I heard a goat and
that I was terribly sorry that I hadn't checked on Abuelita as I
should have. He scolded me severely. But this wasn't enough
punishment, according to my grandmother, so she decided to
penalize me herself by refusing to speak to me. This made me
very sad, and it seemed to affect all of us. **A sense of sorrow and
discomfort permeated our family.**

Two weeks later I asked to go with my father to the big
yellow store in town. While Papá made his purchases I bought a
silver whistle and a long piece of blue satin ribbon. I threaded the
ribbon through the ring on the whistle and tied the ends of the
ribbon together.

....

penalize punish

A sense of sorrow and discomfort permeated our family. We
all felt sad and uncomfortable because of it.

That evening, I placed the whistle in a little box and wrapped it in some colored paper. After supper, I approached my grandmother.

"This is for you, Abuelita. I'm terribly sorry about what happened to you in the shed. I hope you can forgive me."

My grandmother looked at me and said nothing. Then she took the box and opened it. She pulled the whistle out by its ribbon.

"Well, Telésfora, whatever is this for?" she asked, keeping her eyes on the whistle.

"It's to wear around your neck when you are outside. If you need me, just blow the whistle and I'll come to you," I said.

"And how can I be sure you'll hear this little whistle? You couldn't even hear me yelling at you!" But Abuela put it around her neck anyway.

The next evening, while I was feeding the chickens, I heard a faint whistle. I stopped what I was doing and stood very still. Then I heard the whistle more **distinctly**. Yes! It was definitely coming from inside the storage shed. I rushed to the shed and found the door latched. That surprised me because the wind wasn't blowing at all. There was no way that the door could have slammed shut by itself. Something seemed really strange about

....

distinctly clearly

this, and I was suspicious. I unlatched the door and opened it. There stood my grandmother with the whistle in her mouth. She quickly removed it and said, "I think your papá needs to do something about that crazy door latch. Don't you think so, Chatita?"

She hurried out of the shed and we started toward the house. I could see that she was smiling, and I think I even heard her **chuckling**.

....

chuckling laughing

BEFORE YOU MOVE ON...

1. **Setting** Reread pages 24–25. What is it about the setting of Garrapata Road that upsets Keno?

2. **Plot** What is the importance of the whistle in "The Whistle"?

The Gift of Tranquilino Trujillo

It was on **our washday** that Tranquilino Trujillo came into our lives, or should I say, crawled into our lives? It was very early on a Saturday morning in September. My mother and I were home alone, rubbing clothes on scrub boards in big tubs under the tallow tree in the backyard.

I heard Mamá gasp and say, "Chatita, look! Is that a man crawling on the ground? Do you see him? Right there, by the chicken coop!" She pointed at something that definitely seemed to be crawling toward us.

I stood motionless for a few seconds as I attempted to make sense out of what I saw. Meanwhile, my mother grabbed up some towels and rushed over to a body that now lay **immobile** on the ground. It was indeed a man, a very old man, who was bleeding **profusely** from a gash in his scalp. My mother wrapped the

....

our washday the day that we did our laundry
immobile not moving
profusely heavily

towels around his head and told me to fetch some spiderwebs so she could stop the bleeding.

"And bring me a bucket of clean water," she called to me as I gathered webs from inside the privy. "This poor man is covered in so much blood I can't even see his face."

The man appeared to be in great pain and responded to my mother's touch with moans and grimaces. Occasionally he would say, "*Gracias. Dios te bendiga, hija.* Thank you. May God bless you, daughter." But it was difficult to understand his speech because he had no teeth and he seemed to be a *tartamudo*, a stutterer.

Mamá placed the spiderwebs on the gash and continued to **labor over** the man, soothing him with her soft words and cleansing the blood from his head and face. When the bleeding stopped, I helped her take the stranger into our house.

"We'll have to put him in your room for now," Mamá said as she motioned for me to pull back the bedcovers.

We undressed the small man. His body was **gaunt, wizened, and dark**. His thick gray beard grew out in many directions from his chin, giving him a **wild and savage** look. He shivered as we washed his wrinkled skin. Because some of his dried blood had stuck his shirt to his skin, we had to carefully peel it from his chest while he winced in pain. He had bruises, cuts, and scrapes

....

labor over help, clean
gaunt, wizened, and dark skinny, wrinkled, and dark-skinned
wild and savage fierce and scary

all over his body. My mother said that he probably had broken ribs, too.

"He really needs to have that gash in his scalp sewn up. I'll just do what I can to clean it for now," Mamá said as she tied his long gray hair back with a shoelace.

"What do you suppose happened to him?" I asked.

"I don't know. Maybe he was beaten or maybe hit by a vehicle." Mamá began to clean around his head injury with Watkins salve. "Heat some water, Chatita, and make him a little **tea of** *yerbaniz* so he can be calmed."

After I prepared the tea, Mamá told me to tear one of the old bedsheets into strips so she could **bind** the man's chest. I also brought some **sprigs of mugwort** to sweep over his body to rid him of the *susto*, the great fright that was undoubtedly affecting him.

I helped Mamá bind the man, then we dressed him in one of my father's big flannel work shirts. The man drank some of the tea, thanking us and asking God to bless us between every sip. He soon fell into a deep sleep and my mother and I went to wash our dirty clothes. We also washed the old man's clothing.

In the evening, my father came home tired and hungry, and **the last thing he wanted to hear was** that there was a

....

tea of *yerbaniz* herbal tea
bind wrap them around
sprigs of mugwort special herbs
the last thing he wanted to hear was was furious

half-naked stranger asleep in my bed. After Papá took a look at the sleeping man, he took Mamá by the elbow and **steered** her outside. I followed them.

"Chencha! What were you thinking? Don't you realize what you've done? Do you know what that man is?"

But before my mother could reply, my father answered his own questions as he always did when he was angry.

"That man is a *gitano*! A gypsy! You took in a gypsy! Were you thinking it would be nice to invite **a gypsy** to live with us so he could steal everything we own? My God, Chencha, what will the neighbors think?" My father wiped the spittle from the corners of his mouth with his blue bandana and scowled at Mamá.

"And how do you know he is a gypsy? Just what exactly tells you that this man is a gypsy?" my mother demanded to know. She pulled the hairpins from her hair and shook her head until her hair hung loosely.

My father wiped the sweat from his face with his bandana. "Because he is not from around here. And there is an encampment of gypsies between here and town. They came with the **carnival** that's set up on Canal Road."

A carnival so close to our house! What excitement I felt! I

....

steered took

a gypsy a wanderer

carnival traveling show that has rides and games

loved carnivals! I was just about to ask Papá if I could go when I saw my mother turn and face my father with her hands on her hips and **her eyes narrowed and weasel-like**.

In a slow, determined voice she said, "I don't care if he is a gypsy. He is an old man, a very old man. And he is gravely injured."

My father looked away from her stare and replied, "You shouldn't have done this. I don't like it." He cleared his throat and spat on the ground.

My mother spoke up in a louder voice, "Anselmo, listen to me. I am a **Christian, nothing more, nothing less**. I will do what Christians are supposed to do. Do not expect me to **turn away** an injured person, and especially one that reminds me of my own father. Remember that you wouldn't let me be with him when he was sick and dying last year?" Mamá covered her face with her hands but she didn't cry.

It was true. My father had not allowed my mother to make the five-hour bus trip to San Antonio the last time she was notified that her father was not expected to live. Papá said it was just another trick by my grandmother to get my mother to come. This was the third time in a year that Mamá had been told that her father was dying. Always before, she went to San Antonio and

....

her eyes narrowed and weasel-like an angry look in her eyes
Christian, nothing more, nothing less simple religious person
turn away refuse to help

her father soon recovered. However, **on this last occasion** my grandfather had died. My grandmother had been so angry with my mother for not coming that she buried my grandfather before my mother could get there. Mamá said she would never forgive Papá for not allowing her to go to her father.

Mamá placed her hands back on her hips and stared at my father.

"Well, the *gitano* can stay tonight," Papá said, "but tomorrow, I want him out of this house."

"**We'll see**," Mamá answered and stepped back into the house.

But the *gitano* did not leave the next day. The poor old man could not move. He felt terrible pain if any part of his body was touched or moved. He was able to tell us that his name was Tranquilino Trujillo and he was from a town in Mexico called Venado in the state of San Luis Potosí. He had come to Texas to join his daughter and son-in-law who had been working in the Brownsville area. On arriving in Brownsville, he learned that they had gone to Laredo to work.

Don Tranquilino had not had enough money for a bus ticket all the way to Laredo, so he rode the bus as far as El Tule, the little town near our place. Tranquilino had attempted to find work at the carnival on Canal Road, but soon after, he had been

....

on this last occasion this last time
We'll see We will wait and see what happens

attacked by several men and then beaten with **clubs** when they found out that he had no money for them to steal.

"I was left on the side of the road to die. **The dogs would have eaten me**, but the stars showed me the way to you," he said to my mother. "I saw the stars all falling from the sky. They fell on your house, so I followed them. On my hands and knees, I crawled to you. You have saved my life, *m'ija*." Tranquilino smiled and patted my mother's arm.

Mamá said that she liked it when don Tranquilino called her *m'ija*, my daughter. She began to spend as much time as she could caring for him. She made the old man hot tea and chicken and rice soup. She cleansed his wounds several times a day and rubbed Watkins salve on the bad cut on his scalp. She also cut his hair and trimmed his beard.

When my brothers were home, Mamá would have them take don Tranquilino out to sit in the high-back wicker chair under the Chinese tallow tree. She and the old man would talk for hours at a time. He would tell my mother about his life in Mexico. Don Tranquilino had been **a miner** for many years, but one day he had been injured in an explosion and could no longer work as before.

My mother seemed to enjoy caring for don Tranquilino. She

....

clubs heavy sticks; weapons

The dogs would have eaten me I would have died

a miner employed as a person who digs up minerals from the ground

laughed a lot and sang as she worked around the house. I had not seen her this happy in a long time. Almost every day, Papá told Mamá that don Tranquilino seemed well enough to leave, but Mamá always replied that the old man needed just a few more days before she would let him go. This made Papá angry.

He would say to Mamá, "What? You want to give him a few more days to steal more from us? You can't trust gypsies, woman! Why are you so **stubborn**?"

My mother usually did not respond, so Papá would answer his own questions. When Mamá did respond, their arguments would always end with the same results: Papá would go out to his tractor shed and stay for hours, and Mamá would make tea for herself and don Tranquilino.

When the weather became cooler, Papá would come to the kitchen often for cups of hot coffee. My mother and don Tranquilino were usually sitting at the kitchen table drinking *yerbaniz* tea. At first, Papá would sit with them at the table and listen to their conversations, occasionally saying something to the older man. But as time passed, my father **interacted** more with don Tranquilino. Eventually, it seemed to me that the two men shared a **genuine** liking for one another. At some point, Papá decided that don Tranquilino was not a gypsy who had

....

stubborn unwilling to make him leave
interacted spoke
genuine real, honest

come to rob us. My father **even went so far as to congratulate** my mother on the good job she had done in caring for the injured stranger.

Don Tranquilino must have thought my mother had special healing ability because I heard him say one day, "Chencha, *m'ija*, you have a *don*, a gift from God."

"Whatever do you mean? What kind of talent has God given me?"

"You have the ability to nurse the sick back to health, the gift of healing."

My mother laughed. "I don't think it's a gift. I do what my mother before me did, and her mother before her. I do what I can for others."

"Of course," answered don Tranquilino, "but, above all, you must not forget to heal yourself."

As the weeks went by, don Tranquilino grew stronger. He no longer had to be carried, but could walk slowly on his **spindly** legs. He enjoyed sitting in the wicker chair under the tallow tree during the warmer part of the day. But he spent most of his time

---

even went so far as to congratulate changed the way he felt so much that he congratulated

spindly tall and thin

sitting at the table drinking tea and conversing with Mamá as she **went about** her chores in the kitchen.

One day in December, don Tranquilino told Mamá that he thought the time was approaching that he would have to leave us. She responded that it would be a sad time for her, that she would miss him, but she would remember him with much fondness. She told him that she had enough money saved and that she would buy him a bus ticket to Laredo. She even offered to give him some of my brothers' **outgrown** shirts and trousers to take with him.

Don Tranquilino did not leave on the bus. He died that same afternoon, sitting in the wicker chair under the Chinese tallow tree. Upon his death, my mother began sobbing and wailing and could not be **consoled** by my father, my brothers, or by me. She cried all that night and all the next day. Because don Tranquilino had no money and no relatives near by, my father turned his corpse over to the county for burial. My family and I were the only people attending the brief graveside funeral. Mamá wept all through the burial as she would have cried at her own father's funeral. She continued crying after we returned home, and she cried while she and I cleaned my little room removing from our house all reminders that Tranquilino Trujillo had ever been there.

....

went about did
outgrown old
consoled comforted

When we had finished, she finally stopped crying. She and I walked out to the shed where my father was adding oil to the **crankcase** of his tractor.

"Anselmo, I want to tell you something," she said to my father.

My father turned toward her and wiped his hands on his bandana.

She walked up to him, laid her hand on his arm, and said, "I forgive you."

....

crankcase engine

Chatita's Night Out

My first boyfriend was Pete Paloma. I had fallen madly in love with him when I was in the eighth grade. He was handsome in his starched khaki pants and white cotton dress shirt unbuttoned far enough down his chest so that I could see the small gold cross hanging from his neck. Pete had wavy black hair, always slathered with La Parrot brilliantine and combed up into a pompadour. I **was especially attracted to** his smile, showing two big front teeth with a gap between them and through which he spat from time to time.

He didn't know at first that I loved him, and of course I could never have told him. That would have been **improper**. But I could tell his sister, Nilda, and of course she would tell him for me. She and I conveniently became best friends. Nilda liked my brother Keno, so we would occasionally visit back and forth in each other's homes hoping to get a glimpse of or a few words

....

was especially attracted to really loved
improper wrong, unacceptable

with the **objects of our schoolgirl desires**.

By the time I was a sophomore in high school and Pete was a senior, we were in love and had **pledged our undying devotion** to one another. But that's about all it was, just talk. We couldn't hold hands and we sure couldn't kiss. We couldn't even manage to be totally alone. I was not allowed to go out on dates or have suitors come to the house. My goodness no! What would don Tacho and don Chacho think? And what about don Chente and don Cheto, and not forgetting don Kiko and don Lito and don Sixto and don Fito? We couldn't have those noble neighbors thinking badly of don Anselmo Chávez's only daughter. So I devised a plan that would allow Pete and me to be alone without my parents or any of our nosy neighbors knowing.

Pete's sister, Nilda, had been home sick from school for two weeks. She **sent word to** me to bring home her assignments from her teachers. On Thursday evening, I told my mother that I needed to take Nilda some assignments and spend some time helping her **to catch up on** school lessons. Then I held my breath.

"Well, I don't know about that, Chatita," my mother said as she smoothed out the wrinkles in a sheet she had just folded. "Perhaps you had better ask your Papá. He doesn't like you going

....

objects of our schoolgirl desires boys we liked
pledged our undying devotion made promises to be loyal
sent word to asked
to catch up on complete

out at night. You know it doesn't look proper."

I went out to the tractor shed and found Papá adjusting the shredder. He stopped and smiled at me. I quickly asked him if I could go to Nilda's house. Before I could even start to hold my breath, he gave me an answer.

"*Pues bien, sí*, I think it is good that you help your friend."

I was so excited that I turned to start back to the house without even saying thank you to Papá. All I could think of was Pete waiting at his house for me and then us going off together in his father's pickup. We had already planned our few hours together. We would go to a movie in Toronjas, a town about thirty miles away, hoping that no one who knew us would be there.

"*Espérate, muchacha.* Wait!" my father called to me.

I turned around but avoided looking at him.

"You need to be home before ten o'clock," he said as he walked toward me.

"*Sí*, Papá," I answered with much relief.

"And, Keno must take you and bring you back home."

I was still relieved. I saw no problem with my brother doing that.

"And," my father continued, "he must wait for you there at

Pues bien, sí It is good, yes (in Spanish)

don Nepo Paloma's house."

That was **disastrous**! Keno would never go along with my plans to go out with Pete. Keno would stop me and tell Papá, and that would ruin everything. But I still thought it was **worth a try**.

While Keno drove me to the Paloma farm, I asked him if he would stay with Nilda while I went to a movie with Pete. He said no because he didn't like Nilda, and besides, he had heard she was in bed with the chicken pox. Seeing that my plans were **now falling apart**, I began to cry.

"Come on, Chatita, don't **bawl**. I can wait somewhere else. I don't have to stay with Nilda Paloma while you and Pete are at a movie."

I could hardly believe what I was hearing!

"But, little sister, you had better be back at Paloma's place before ten o'clock so I can pick you up, or we will both be in lots of trouble with Papá."

Pete was already waiting in his father's old Dodge pickup truck when Keno dropped me off. I gave Pete's little sister, Juana, the assignments for Nilda and asked her to take them in the house to her. I then eagerly got into the vehicle with Pete. The truck rattled and shook, and I was sure I could see pavement through the holes in the floorboard beneath my feet. But I didn't

....

disastrous terrible; not good
worth a try a plan that I should try
now falling apart not working
bawl cry

care about any of that. Pete and I were alone for the first time. I was **giddy with delight**.

"Did you have any trouble getting your father's pickup?" I asked.

"No. He's not even home. He went to Brownsville in his new farm truck."

"Did he go to sell his leftover crops?" I asked.

"No, my father has a *movida*," Pete answered **with a nonchalant tone**.

I gasped. "A girlfriend? Why would he have a girlfriend? Doesn't he love your mom?"

"Of course he loves her. He's good to her," Pete said.

"Well, I think that's terrible, Pete, just terrible."

"I don't see what's so terrible. My father takes good care of us. He pays the bills and buys us things. He's a good man."

"And what if your mother finds out?"

"She already knows."

I had never heard of anything like this before. I thought of my father and mother. What would Mamá do if Papá had a *movida*? She would probably kill him, that is if my grandmother didn't do it first.

---

giddy with delight so happy and excited

with a nonchalant tone in a casual way; like this was not a big deal

It was getting late when Pete and I got out of the movie, so we headed directly for Garrapata Road. We were on a back road about ten miles from the Paloma farm when the pickup stopped running. It didn't **cough, it didn't sputter**, it just stopped.

Pete tried many times to restart it, but it would do nothing. He checked the gasoline. Yes, it had gasoline. He raised the hood, but he couldn't see anything because he didn't have a flashlight. He cursed a little and said we should wait a while before trying to start it again. I was beginning to get frantic. It was already ten o'clock. I wondered how long Keno would wait for me, and I wondered if Papá and Mamá had gone to bed. Maybe they would go to sleep quickly and never know I wasn't there.

Pete tried to start the engine again. Nothing happened. I was feeling **desperate**.

"Come on, Pete! Let's push the pickup." I opened the door to get out.

"Don't be stupid," he replied.

"Well, we should do something. You're not doing anything." I began to cry.

"I think we should just sit here until somebody comes by," Pete said. "Maybe some farmer will be coming home late."

"Well, I hope they hurry up," I replied.

....

cough, it didn't sputter make any sounds
desperate scared; ready to try anything

Pete and I waited a long time in the pickup. We hardly talked. At one point Pete reached over and took my hand, but I was too upset to enjoy his touch. I pulled my hand back and Pete soon went to sleep.

I couldn't sleep. I was too scared thinking about what was going to happen to me when I got home. I was especially concerned about how worried Mamá must be by now and how angry Papá would be, and also Keno. He would be very angry because he would be in trouble with Papá for going along with my **deception**.

By two o'clock no one had come down the road. I started crying again and my sobs awakened Pete. He decided to walk to the Duncan's farm to ask Clarence Duncan for his pickup. I didn't like being left alone, but Pete said he could **make better time** without me.

It was almost daybreak when Pete came back in Clarence's pickup. I told Pete it would be best to let me out a little distance from my house. I did not want him to drive me all the way, but he refused and took me to my house. Papá and Keno were sitting out in front of our house drinking coffee and waiting for me. They watched me get out of Clarence's pickup.

"Well, Telésfora, **what do you have to say for yourself?**"

....

deception lie, plan
make better time get there quicker
what do you have to say for yourself can you explain why you are just coming home now

my father asked, using my real name as he always did when he was angry with me.

"We had trouble with the pickup," I said **meekly**.

"*¡Hija desgraciada!*" my father mumbled.

This made me wince. "I'm sorry, Papá. The pickup broke down."

"And your poor mother is **sick with worry**. And your brother and I are humiliated," my father continued.

Keno spoke up. "Clarence Duncan, of all people, Chatita! You chose to stay out all night with *him?*"

"You know better than that," I replied.

"All I know is what I saw. That was Clarence's pickup you got out of," Keno said.

There was no mistaking that pickup. It was a canary yellow color and had fat brown-skinned hula girls with red hair painted on each door. My father said it was the **tackiest-looking** vehicle in the state of Texas.

"What will don Pancho think? And don Tacho and doña Persíngula?" my father asked, referring to our nearest neighbors. "I'm very disappointed in you, daughter, and I am ashamed of the disgrace you have brought upon this family!"

With that, I turned and ran into the house. My mother was

....

meekly weakly
¡Hija desgraciada! Terrible daughter! (in Spanish)
sick with worry upset and worried
tackiest-looking ugliest

kneeling in prayer at her small bedside altar. She had five candles burning and was praying in a low monotone. She **refused to acknowledge my presence**.

I didn't go to bed because it was almost time to get up and go to school. I couldn't even relax because **my brain wouldn't turn off** thinking about the events of the night. Keno and I needed to talk. I wanted to let him know what had really happened.

After I dressed for school and started to eat breakfast, my father told me to stay home from school. I asked why.

"You must accompany your mamá and me to the Duncan's home. You and that Duncan boy will have to be married because the two of you spent the night together," my father said.

I could not believe what I was hearing! Before I could say anything, Mamá called me into her room and shut the door.

Without looking at me she asked, **"Are you ruined?"**

"Mamá, what do you mean?"

"Holy Mary, Mother of God! You know what I mean!" She turned and looked squarely at me. "Did Clarence Duncan ruin you?"

"Mamá, please believe me! I was not with Clarence! I was with Pedro Paloma. And, no, I am *not* ruined," I answered.

"You were seen with that Duncan boy by your father and

....

refused to acknowledge my presence would not speak to me

my brain wouldn't turn off I could not stop

Are you ruined? Did you do something bad with him?

64

your brother when you got out of his pickup this morning."

"That's not true!" I cried.

"*¡Ay, madrecita!* You were out all night! Keno came home without you! And your friend Nilda said that you were never at her house last night! And she didn't know where you were! And I thought you were dead! And your poor father went everywhere looking for you! *All* the neighbors went looking for you!" My mother took a deep breath, but **broke off her tirade**. "Get ready. We're going to the Duncan's place after breakfast," she said curtly.

All the way to the Duncan farm my parents and I rode without speaking. The only thing on my mind was that ugly, redheaded, freckle-faced **gringo**, Clarence. I would rather die than marry him, but I knew he would tell my parents the truth. Once they saw their terrible mistake they would insist that Pete and I get married and I could **go along with** that.

Mr. Duncan was outside when we arrived. It was easy to see where Clarence got his looks, especially his curly red hair and millions of freckles. He looked just like his father, only Mr. Duncan was bigger and uglier. I looked around, but I didn't see Clarence or his pickup.

"Hello, Mr. Chávez," Mr. Duncan said as he walked over to my father's side of the pickup. He nodded to my mother and me.

....

¡Ay, madrecita! Good heavens! (in Spanish)
broke off her tirade stopped yelling
gringo white person (in Spanish)
go along with agree to

"How are you folks today?"

"Well, not too good to tell you the truth, Mr. Duncan," my father replied. "Your son kept my daughter out all night, which has **compromised her greatly**. I want to know what **his intentions are**."

Mr. Duncan smiled slightly. "Too bad he ain't here to discuss this with you."

Mrs. Duncan came out on the porch with a child on her hip and four children following her. "Anything wrong, Delbert?"

"No, but you need to come out here, Ina Belle, and meet Mr. and Mrs. Chávez."

Clarence's mother slowly approached our pickup. Her thin face looked tired and drawn and she had no teeth that I could see.

"Hello, folks. Do you want to come in?" she asked as she smiled and brushed back a wisp of her oily blond hair.

"Thank you, Mrs. Duncan, but we don't need to come in if Clarence isn't here," my father answered. "But I do want you and your husband to know that because your son kept our daughter out all night, he needs to marry her **to protect her reputation**."

"Oh, is that your daughter there?" Mrs. Duncan asked as she pointed toward me. Some of the children walked around our pickup and looked in the passenger-side window at us. They all

....

compromised her greatly put her in a bad position

his intentions are he plans to do about it

to protect her reputation so that people do not think badly of her

66

had freckles and varying shades of red hair.

"This is my daughter, Telésfora. Clarence brought her home around five o'clock this morning," my father said gravely.

"And Clarence wants to marry her?" Mrs. Duncan said. "How wonderful! Have her pack her things and come on over. It'll be so nice to have another woman around here to help me with the work."

At that Mamá took hold of my arm tightly, as if to say Telésfora is not going anywhere. I **broke down** and began to sob.

Mr. Duncan spoke up immediately. "But Clarence and your daughter were not out together."

"And how do you know this?" asked my father.

"Because Clarence was here with us all night. Pete Paloma came by early this morning and borrowed Clarence's truck because he and your girl broke down in Paloma's old Dodge."

"Are you certain?" my father asked.

"Yep. Pete borrowed my boy's pickup to take the girl home. Clarence is with him now. They've gone to see if they can start Paloma's pickup truck."

"Anselmo, let's go home," my mother said as she thanked Mr. Duncan. "Thank you for your time, Mr. Duncan."

"Glad to help."

....

At that Mamá took hold of When she heard that, Mamá grabbed

broke down got upset

My parents argued all the way home about whether or not Pete Paloma would have to marry me. My mother thought he should because she now was sure that Pete was the one who had kept me out all night. My father thought I should marry Clarence because everyone else thought that I had stayed out all night with him. I had been seen in Clarence's pickup by some of the neighbors. No one was going to believe that Clarence wasn't in that truck.

"Anselmo, those Duncans aren't even Catholic," my mother protested. "I don't want her marrying someone that's not a Christian! At least Pedro Paloma comes from a Catholic family."

My father shook his head. "But that doesn't matter now. What matters is that we protect Chatita's reputation. If our friends and neighbors think she was out all night with Clarence, they won't understand why she's marrying Pedro Paloma. I say Clarence needs to marry her. What will don Tacho think?"

Don Tacho would have thought that my father was crazy. I certainly did! Someone needed to **put a stop to all of this lunacy**. Finally, Keno **stepped in** and told my parents that perhaps they should rethink all of this. He took responsibility for me going to

....

put a stop to all of this lunacy calm my father down; tell my parents that I did not have to marry anyone

stepped in spoke up; interrupted

the movie with Pete by telling my parents that he had given me permission to go. He apologized eloquently to my parents. They were angry with him, but they finally calmed down.

On Monday, Nilda got on the school bus and sat down beside me as usual, except this time she had an unfriendly look on her face.

"Well, you've really done it now, Chatita Chávez," she said. "You've caused my brother to leave home and join the Army. If he gets killed, it'll be your fault, and I'll never forgive you and neither will my parents!"

It was true. When Pete found out from the Duncans what my parents were planning for the boy who kept me out all night, he got scared and decided to join the Army. I was a little upset **at his abrupt departure**, but I was sure he'd come back for me as soon as he finished his basic training.

He didn't. When he finished his **hitch** in the Army, I thought he would come back for me, but he did not even come to greet me. From time to time I would hear about him, and occasionally I would get a glimpse of him. This always excited me and the old feelings I had for him would **flare up**. I knew that I wasn't over him. Then I heard that he married a girl from Port Lavaca. He lived up there for several years, then someone told me that he had

....

at his abrupt departure that he left so suddenly
hitch time
flare up come back

come back to Garrapata Road to live.

It was probably in the summer of 1954 that Pete and I finally saw one another at a wedding celebration. We talked a short while and before we **parted**, Pete asked if he could see me again.

"What do you mean by see me again?" I asked, hoping that after all this time we would finally **get together**.

"Well, you know what I mean. I'd like to take you out on a date. You're really looking good, Chatita. I want to get to know you again."

"Pete! You're still married, right?" I asked, thinking that he would say no.

"Of course I'm still married. And I'm a good husband. I'm good to my wife, I pay all the bills, and I buy her nice things."

That was the **end of** Pete Paloma. I **was finally over him**.

....

parted said good-bye
get together start dating
end of last time I saw
was finally over him did not love him anymore

BEFORE YOU MOVE ON...

1. **Character's Motive** Reread page 55. Why does Mamá forgive Papá for forcing her to miss being with her father when he died?

2. **Plot** Why do Mamá and Papá insist that Chatita marry the boy who kept her out all night?

II

The Bermúdez Family

Her Brother's Keeper

"Zulema, you need to finish your work." It was Mrs. Humbolt speaking to me.

"Zulema, did you hear me? You need to hurry and do those problems before the bell rings," she said a little louder.

"Yes, Miss," I responded and smiled at my eighth grade teacher while picking up my pencil. All day it had been difficult for me to concentrate on schoolwork. I had had a slight headache since the morning. How nice it would be to go home, take off my sweaty dress, and lie down for a while.

When the **dismissal** bell rang, I turned in my incomplete assignment and left the classroom. I hurried to get on the bus that would take me to our farm on Garrapata Road about five miles away from the school. My head was beginning to throb with pain, and as I boarded the bus, I felt **a pang of nausea**. Before I reached my assigned seat, I realized that my little

....

dismissal last
a pang of nausea sick to my stomach

brother was not on the bus.

"Paco, Paco? Where's Paco?" I asked the students who were already seated.

No one had seen him. I got off the bus and looked up and down the rows of school buses as I called out his name. Our bus driver, Toribio, was standing nearby talking to another driver.

"Have you seen Paco?" I asked him.

"No. He hasn't come out yet," Toribio replied.

Some of the buses at the front of the line were already starting their engines. I didn't know what to do. I could not leave without Paco. He was only six years old and would not know how to get home without me. My mother would **never forgive me** if I didn't bring him home.

"Why don't you go to his classroom and see if he's still there?" Toribio suggested. "And hurry. I can't wait very long."

I rushed into the school building and down the hall to Paco's classroom. No one was there. I thought that he probably went next door to my building, so I went there. I found no one in the **deserted** halls or in the classrooms. All of the teachers were outside helping their students on the buses.

I hurried back to the school bus. Toribio was ready to pull away. He opened the door and said, "Paco hasn't come and I can't

....

never forgive me be furious
deserted empty

wait any longer. Why don't you go to the principal's office. They can help you there."

This had never happened to me before. I was afraid. We did not have a telephone at our house. None of our neighbors on Garrapata Road had telephones, so I could not call home. But I was determined to find Paco.

I decided to look in the elementary building again. The deserted building was frightening. My footsteps echoed in the **high corridors** as I ran from classroom to classroom, upstairs and downstairs.

This was a place where I did not want to be. I didn't feel safe here, not now, not anytime. My parents made me come to school so I could get educated because they never did. But I didn't like school. The teachers had so many rules and I couldn't remember them all. I was afraid of some of the teachers. They scolded me if they heard me speaking Spanish. Didn't they realize I couldn't help it? Sometimes the other students made fun of me, especially the **town girls**. They weren't very friendly. They laughed at me because I brought Paco's and my lunch to school in a lard can.

---

high corridors large hallways
town girls rich girls who lived in town

A lot of the town children brought their lunches in brown paper bags. We seldom had paper bags.

* * *

Paco wasn't in any of the classrooms so I had to look in the **damp, sour-smelling toilets**. Next, I talked to the janitor who was sweeping the hall. He said that because it was Friday, everyone would be going home early and that I should look outside. I made two rounds outside the building, but I didn't see Paco.

It was time to **notify** someone who would do something to help me, so I went to the principal's office hoping to find someone there. My head was really hurting and I was **on the verge of** crying. I didn't see the principal, but I did see his secretary, Mrs. Thacker, seated at her desk.

She looked up at me. "You need to go on home. Students aren't allowed in the building after four o'clock. You know that."

She could have at least asked me if she could help me, but no, she scolded me. "Please, ma'am. Help me. I can't go home without my little brother. I can't find him anywhere!"

"Well, you'll just have to call your parents." She peered at me over her glasses and pursed her lips.

....

damp, sour-smelling toilets bathrooms that smelled gross
notify tell
on the verge of about to start

"I can't, ma'am. We don't have a telephone."

"And what is your name?"

"Zulema Bermúdez."

"And what's your brother's name?"

"Paco Bermúdez. Well, it's really Francisco Bermúdez."

"Where do you live?" she asked.

"On Garrapata Road."

"Umm, I've never heard of it," she answered and turned back to the work on her desk.

I slumped down in a nearby chair and began to cry.

"My goodness, child. **It can't be that bad!**" Mrs. Thacker said.

"I don't know what to do," I said between my sobs. "My little brother came to school on the bus with me this morning and now I can't find him and he wasn't on the bus this afternoon and the bus left without us and I feel so bad."

"Well, quit crying, child. That does not help in anything. Go look for him," Mrs. Thacker said as she motioned for me to get up. "Have you checked all the classrooms?"

"Yes, in both buildings, upstairs and downstairs, and even in the toilets."

"What about the **clinic**?" she asked and rose from her chair.

....

It can't be that bad! I am sure your brother is fine!

clinic nurse's office

She took a large ring of keys from a hook on the wall.

I followed her down the hall to the clinic where she had trouble getting the key to open the lock. The room was dark and I couldn't see anything. I stepped inside the windowless room that was very warm and musty. Mrs. Thacker switched on a light. I noticed a large screen standing in the corner, so I walked over to look behind it. There on a **cot** lay my sleeping brother. His face **appeared flush** and dry. He began to **whimper** when I awoke him.

"Well, you're certainly lucky that I had work that kept me here late today," Mrs. Thacker said. "Otherwise your little brother may have stayed in this room all weekend."

"Oh, how awful!" I said as I put my arms around Paco.

"It could have easily happened. The janitor has already cleaned and locked up everything on this floor. He probably would have never even heard your brother crying for help," Mrs. Thacker said. "I guess someone forgot he was here. That's too bad."

"Thank you, ma'am," I said and smiled at her, hoping she would offer to give us a ride home.

Paco was crying and hugging me. It was obvious that he was sick. His eyes were glassy and I could feel that his head was really

....

cot portable bed
appeared flush was red
whimper cry

warm. But Mrs. Thacker didn't seem to notice when she said, "Well, children, you'd better start walking home before your mother gets worried about you."

There was no choice for me but to start the long walk home. Paco leaned on me and we **stumbled along as best we could**.

"What happened, Paquito? Why were you asleep in the clinic?" I asked him as we headed down the street.

"I got sick. My teacher wasn't at school today. Some other teacher put me in the clinic," he answered and his little body trembled.

"I guess she forgot about you," I said.

I held him as tightly as I could against my body. I wished I **had the strength** to carry him. It was going to be a long walk to our farm. We had not reached the **outskirts** of town and Paco could not even walk. My head hurt more than it had ever hurt before. I really hoped someone we knew would come by and give us a ride. As we were passing Gordon's Grocery I remembered that our neighbor, Clarence Duncan, sometimes worked for Mr. Gordon. Paco and I went into the store and I immediately saw Clarence cleaning produce bins.

"Sure, I'll give you a ride home, but I don't have my truck. My dad is coming for me at eight tonight. If you'll wait, we'll take

....

stumbled along as best we could walked as fast as we could
had the strength was strong enough
outskirts border

you home," Clarence said and wiped his hands on the big green apron he was wearing.

"Thank you, but we can't wait. My mother is going to be too worried about us," I said.

It wasn't five o'clock yet. I didn't want to wait until eight. My mother would be crazy with worry. Paco was getting worse. I told Clarence that we'd better go on but to give us some water before we left.

"You don't look so well yourself, Zulema," Clarence said as he gave Paco a drink of cool water. I thanked Clarence, put Paco on my back, and headed out of town on the road that would take us home.

A number of vehicles came by, two even honked at us, but no one stopped to help us. Paco moaned a lot in my ear as I **trudged along** with him hanging on my back. I didn't like the idea of being out on the road after dark. I knew my mother would be sick with worry, so I walked as fast as I could. A few times Paco got down and walked along beside me. But I could go faster with him on my back.

It was after dark when we arrived home. To my dismay, the house was dark and our pickup truck was gone. Perhaps my worried parents were out looking for us. The thought of my poor

....

trudged along walked slowly

grieving mother was terrible. But if my parents were looking for us, why hadn't they seen us on the road?

I lit the kitchen **lantern** and got Paco ready for bed. He was shivering and telling me he was cold. I noticed that his face had reddened and he was hot. He said his head hurt him. I put him in bed and put a wet cloth on his forehead. Then I lay down beside him in the dark bedroom and put a wet cloth on my forehead. I wanted to go to sleep, but I was too worried about my mother. How I wished she were home. I was concerned about Paco's sickness. He needed Mamá. I needed her, too.

I was almost asleep when I heard my father's truck pull into the yard. My mother got out and came into the house and I heard my father drive out to the tractor shed.

"Zulema, we're home," my mother called from the kitchen. "Are you already in bed?"

"Yes, I'm here with Paquito," I answered. "He's asleep."

"Why haven't you cooked some supper? Your father and I are very tired and hungry," my mother said. "I've been over at your Uncle Zenovio's all afternoon and evening. I was helping your Aunt Prudencia because all four children have the red measles. It's a terrible illness. It usually comes in the spring." My mother continued talking as she took pots and pans out of the cupboard.

....

grieving sad
lantern light in its protective case

"My goodness, Zulema, how can I cook anything with a cold stove? Why couldn't you have at least warmed it for me?"

I heard her **chunking wood** into the stove.

"Mamá, please come here," I called. "I need you."

She stopped what she was doing and stepped to the bedroom doorway.

"What is it?" she asked.

"I'm worried about Paco. He's sick."

My mother stepped back into the kitchen for the lantern and returned to look at Paco.

She bent over him holding the lantern so she could see him. "Oh, dear. I'm afraid he has the measles. I hope it won't **be an epidemic like** two years ago." She removed the cloth from his head and went to the kitchen for a small basin of water. Then she returned to replace the wet cloth on Paco's forehead.

"And you. Why do you have a cloth on your forehead?" she asked me as she reached down and felt my face.

"I have a headache," I said as I sat up. I began to talk and cry at the same time, telling her **of the terrible ordeal** Paco and I had been through.

She took the wet cloth from my forehead and began to wash my face. She listened quietly as I told her again about what

....

chunking wood breaking the wood into pieces and throwing it

be an epidemic like spread as fast as it did

of the terrible ordeal about the terrible things

had happened.

"I'm so sorry. If your father and I had been home, we would have gone looking for you as soon as we noticed that the school bus had passed without letting you off," she said. She hugged me and replaced the wet cloth on my forehead.

"I'm proud of you, Zulema," she said quietly.

Paco and I both had the measles and we spent the next ten days in bed in a darkened room. I must have been sicker than Paco because Mamá seemed to **hover over** me just a little more. And she gave me lots of hugs and smiles along with delicious chicken soup and lemon grass tea.

....

hover over watch and take care of

BEFORE YOU MOVE ON...

1. **Inference** Reread page 77 and think about the story called "The Dancing Queens of Garrapata Road." Why hasn't Mrs. Thacker heard of Garrapata Road?

2. **Comparisons** Compare how Zulema is treated at school to how she is treated at home.

La Tamalada

I remember being a happy ten-year-old boy that December in 1942 when I heard my abuela say to Mamá, "Daughter, you need to tell Tacho to kill a hog. I want to start making **tamales**."

"But it's a little early, don't you think? It's two weeks until Christmas," my mother answered as she stopped in the middle of rolling a tortilla.

Abuela was sitting at the kitchen table cleaning beans. She looked up from her work and replied. "But Agustín is home from his Army training. Who knows how soon he'll be going off to the war? We need to make tamales now."

"Yes, I know," Mamá sighed, wiping her eyes with the hem of her apron. She seemed to do that a lot lately when anyone talked about my two oldest brothers.

"First Pancracio joins the Army and now Agustín will be going." Mamá sighed again and continued rolling the tortilla.

....

tamales food made of cornmeal and meat that is wrapped in cornhusks (in Spanish)

"*Bueno*, I'll tell Tacho to have one of the hogs butchered for you."

Whenever Abuela got the ***ganas*** to do something, no one could stop her. I knew that she would soon begin the *tamalada*, and many of our neighbors from up and down Garrapata Road would be coming to help make those delicious tamales that were said to be the best for miles around. My big concern at that moment, however, was which hog Papá would kill. We had two male adult pigs and several **shoats**. Pánfilo was the biggest pig on our farm. But to use him for the tamales! I was mortified to think that Papá would kill my pig.

Later that same day I heard Mamá tell Abuela, "It will **break Paco's heart**, but it must be done. I wish he didn't like that pig so much."

What would break my heart? Were Mamá and Abuela talking about butchering Pánfilo for their tamales? I couldn't bear to think of having my pig eaten. And I could never eat even a mouthful of him, not one tamal, not one *chicharrón*, not even one delicious pork rib.

I wondered if I would be able to save my pig from Gumercindo, our Mexican hired hand who killed the hogs for Papá. I had already saved Pánfilo from sure death on the day he was born. He was the **runt** of a litter of seventeen piglets.

....

ganas desire (in Spanish)
shoats young pigs
break Paco's heart upset Paco
runt smallest and weakest

It would have been impossible for such a scrawny little pig to survive. On the day he had been born, I stood on the bottom rail of the pigpen looking over at the **sow** and her piglets while my father inspected the litter.

Papá picked up an almost lifeless piglet and said, "Too bad about this little one. He will surely die. He needs to be disposed of."

"Yes, don Tacho, it's too bad. I'll throw him in the *bote*," said Gumercindo as he took the piglet from Papá.

"No, Papá, wait," I cried out. "Please don't throw him in the trash barrel. Let me try to feed him."

"I'm afraid **he's too far gone**," Papá answered, taking the piglet out of Gumercindo's hand. "But go ahead. Ask Abuela for a rubber nipple."

I gently took the little pig from Papá and ran to Abuela. I found her in the house and I quickly told her what I needed and why. She laughed at me and poked at the piglet with her crooked index finger. She gave me one of the red rubber nipples that she used from time to time for orphaned animals. She told me not to be disappointed because one could not always be successful with runts, especially pigs.

Mamá observed all of this and said to Abuela, "Mamá, don't

....

sow mother pig
he's too far gone he is too sick

encourage Paco to keep that piglet. They're such dirty animals. Besides, it will just die anyway."

"Persíngula, don't talk like that," Abuela responded. "You don't know if it will die. Paquito **has a gift with** animals. He always helps me when I try to save **God's little creatures**."

"Mamá, death is God's way," my mother answered. "Every animal that is born cannot be expected to live. There are always more born than need to survive. That's God's plan," she said.

I noticed a sad look on Mamá's face, the one that she usually reserved for the times when she talked about her own three babies who had died.

Then Mamá turned to me. "Paco, I don't want that pig in this house. Take it out now."

I started toward the door. Mamá continued, "And if that pig does live, don't come crying to me when we butcher it. We raise these pigs to eat and sell. Remember that, son."

I put the nipple on an empty RC Cola bottle that I took from the tub where we kept the **returnables**. I now had a good way to feed the piglet that I named Pánfilo. During the day he stayed in a box with a hot water bottle. Abuela fed the pig and kept the water bottle warm. At night Pánfilo slept next to me in the little sleeping house I shared with my brothers. He was a lot of trouble

....

has a gift with knows how to take care of
God's little creatures animals
returnables recyclables; used bottles

wanting to suck the nipple all the time. Poor Pánfilo made lots of noise with his squealing, snorting, grunting, and belching. My brother Agustín patted my pig every morning and called him *puerco*, but never complained about him. On the other hand, my brother Benny complained to Mamá that he couldn't sleep because of Pánfilo, so Mamá **banished the piglet from** the sleeping house. But I wasn't defeated. The pig and I joined Gumercindo at night out in the tractor shed. Gumercindo lent me his extra *petate* and blanket, so I made myself a bed on the ground next to his. Gumercindo made so much noise himself snoring that I'm sure he never heard one little squealing pig.

With a lot of help, that pig managed to survive, and he ate better than most pigs. When Gumercindo finished milking our cow, I would swipe some of the warm frothy milk for Pánfilo. Sometimes my grandmother would skim off some of the cream for the pig when Mamá wasn't looking. I brought him the best food from out of the hogs' slop bucket before Gumercindo took it out to the pen. My big sister Zulema often fed Pánfilo things like raw eggs and butter, which if Mamá had found out **would have meant good-bye forever to** Pánfilo.

It was apparent that the pig **took a liking to** me. He followed me around the farm everywhere. Agustín said that Pánfilo acted

....

puerco dirty, pig (in Spanish)
banished the piglet from would not allow the pig in
would have meant good-bye forever to she would have killed
took a liking to liked, loved

like a dog. Benny said that Pánfilo was ugly and that his dull black hair made him look like he had **dog mange**. He never had the mange. He did run with the dogs and played with the dogs. He even ate with the dogs when they would let him. Every afternoon as I walked toward home down Garrapata Road from the school bus stop, our three dogs and Pánfilo would come running down the road to greet me.

Occasionally Pánfilo would follow me into the house. If my mother saw him she would yell at me, "Francisco Javier, get that pig out of the house or he will wake up tomorrow in my big black pot!"

I really never thought she meant this until that day in December when I heard her and my abuela talking about killing a hog to make tamales. I wasn't sure if it was my pig that had been selected for the *tamalada* until I overheard Mamá tell Papá to butcher Pánfilo.

"But Persíngula, think about the boy," Papá said to Mamá. "Paco and that pig are friends. We have other pigs we can butcher."

Mamá responded, "They are all too small. Besides, that pig called Pánfilo is getting to be too fat. He needs to be eaten now. So I want that pig butchered."

....

dog mange a skin disease

"No, not the boy's pig," my father pleaded.

"Listen to me," my mother said sternly. "The boy knew from the beginning that we would someday eat that pig. That day is quickly coming. And, my dear husband, if you want tamales for Agustín before he goes to war, you will kill the pig tomorrow."

"*¡Ay!* My dear wife, our butcher, Gumercindo, is not here," said Papá as he smiled at Mamá. "Have you forgotten that?"

It was true that Gumercindo had been called back to Mexico to help his brother who had been injured. My father had temporarily hired a new helper named Serapio, but he was not nearly as helpful as Gumercindo.

"I said, have you forgotten that Gumercindo is not here," Papá said to my mother.

"I know where Gumercindo is," my mother **retorted**. "Find someone to kill the animal. Or kill it yourself."

What happened immediately after that is somewhat **muddled** in my memory. I do recall talking to my abuela. She said, "*¡Ay de mí!* Paquito, you may have to sacrifice Pánfilo."

Afterward I went out to the sleeping house where Agustín was unpacking his things for his brief visit with us. I talked to him about my fear that Pánfilo would be butchered. I told him what our grandmother had said about sacrificing Pánfilo.

....

retorted replied angrily

muddled unclear

"What did she mean, sacrifice?" I asked Agustín.

My brother laid his hand on the top of my head and said, "Sacrifice means to give up something that **you hold dear**, something that you don't want to live without."

"Do you think killing Pánfilo is a sacrifice?" I asked.

Agustín sat without speaking for a few moments and then said, "Pánfilo is your pig. Only you will know if his death is a sacrifice."

I didn't really understand this, and I began to cry. Agustín took me in his arms and held me for a long time. I don't remember going to my bed that night. Perhaps I fell asleep in Agustín's arms.

The next morning I awoke early to the sounds of knives being sharpened and wood being chopped for the fire pits. I saw my abuela adding white powdered lime to the water in a *paila*, the big black cauldron that sat over a roaring fire. I knew she would use that water to make the hair easier to scrape off of the pig. Then I saw Pánfilo tied to a post. There was no mistake about it. He was to be butchered. I hid under the *guallín* so no one would see me crying. I often hid under the big wagon when I was upset. I saw Papá and Serapio approach Pánfilo. Serapio had a small **caliber rifle** in his hand.

"Now remember, make sure the bullet goes in directly in the

....

you hold dear you love; is very important to you
small caliber rifle gun

middle of the forehead. Wait until he's **down good**, then plunge the knife into his heart," Papá told Serapio. "Are you certain that you know how to do this?"

"Oh, yes, Don Tacho. Please do not worry. I've done this many times," a somewhat arrogant Serapio responded as he **checked the safety on** the rifle.

Before Serapio could raise the rifle to Pánfilo's head, my sister Zulema came running out of the house yelling, "Wait, wait! Don't **stick** him yet! You don't have the plug!"

She walked over to the *desgranadora* and bent over a pile of dried corncobs. She chose one and wrapped it in a white piece of flannel cloth. Then she took it to Serapio.

"My mother will be very angry if you let this pig lose his blood out on the ground. She wants all the blood for making *morcilla*."

"Yes, of course. The blood pudding," Serapio answered. "So when I shoot him, I stick this dry *olote* in the bullet hole?" Serapio seemed puzzled as he looked at the corncob.

Papá spoke up, "No, after you drive the knife into his heart, pull the knife out and plug that hole with the corncob. Are you sure you know what you are doing?"

Serapio didn't answer. He dropped the corncob, raised the

....

down good fallen on the ground; shot
checked the safety on prepared
stick cut, stab

rifle, and shot Pánfilo in the head. My poor pig flopped to the ground and after **a couple of jerks** he lay still. I watched in horror as Serapio took a knife from its **scabbard** and plunged it into my pig's body. Pánfilo jumped up squealing and the rope came loose from his neck. Pánfilo **took off running** across my father's carrot field with the knife dangling from his body. I came out from under the *guallín* and chased Pánfilo.

Serapio raised the rifle and yelled at me, "Get out of the way, boy. Let me **get a shot at** him!"

I ran in behind Pánfilo, staying between him and Serapio and yelling, "Go Pánfilo, go! *¡Ándale! ¡Corre, corre!* Hurry! Run, run!"

And how he did run! He ran straight for the thicket that grew next to our farm. I lost sight of him somewhere in all that growth of weeds, *mezquite, huisache*, and cactus, and Pánfilo lost the poorly placed knife. I was overjoyed and hoped that my pig would run all day and all night and never come home.

When I got back to the house my father was already in his pickup truck.

"Come on, son. Let's go find that poor pig!" he said to me as I climbed into the vehicle.

We looked all through the thicket, but saw nothing. We

....

a couple of jerks a few movements
scabbard holder
took off running ran
get a shot at shoot

drove up and down Garrapata Road, stopping at all the farms. No one had seen Pánfilo, which made me happy. We searched **adjacent** roads, looking and inquiring about my pig. We **had no luck in finding** the animal.

My mother was furious at Serapio for being **an inept** pig killer, but she was more furious at Papá for giving the task to the **unproven hired hand** in the first place.

"That hog is worth a lot of money, and the two of you have lost it!" she yelled at the men. "Two grown men, and neither of you can kill one little pig! I should have asked Benito and Agustín to kill that hog!" she added. "My boys could have done a better job than the two of you. Even Zulema could have killed that hog. You two are pitiful butchers! I think you couldn't even kill a cockroach!" she concluded as she marched out to the privy where she stayed for several hours until she calmed down.

Later that evening Don Anselmo Chávez came to tell my father that someone had seen a grizzly looking hog at the Duncan's place. It was seen standing near Duncan's equipment shed where it was probably tied up. Maybe that was the pig my father had been looking for most of the day.

My mother overheard this and told my father, "You go right now and demand that Mr. Duncan give us our hog."

....

adjacent nearby
had no luck in finding could not find
an inept a bad
unproven hired hand new worker

I was a little afraid of the Duncan boys, but I went with my father anyway to see if Pánfilo was really at the Duncan's place.

Mr. Duncan came out on his front porch with about five little kids following him. My father stepped out of the pickup and asked about the pig, but Mr. Duncan said he hadn't seen it.

"Well, **do you mind** if I look around?" my father asked.

"Yes, I do mind because I said I haven't seen your hog. It's not here. You'll just have to **take my word for it**," Mr. Duncan stated as he took several steps toward my father.

Papá got back into the truck and cursed all the way back to our house. He told me he knew Pánfilo was hidden in Duncan's shed and that we would never see that pig again. He called Mr. Duncan a lot of really bad names.

Early the next morning the Duncan's redheaded freckle-faced son, Clarence, knocked on our front door. He had a rope in his hand that was attached to my pig. Pánfilo looked very much alive and especially well fed.

"Is this here your hog, Mr. Bermúdez?" Clarence asked my father. "If it is, my daddy said to give it to you and to no one else but you."

"Yes, it's mine," said Papá as he took the rope from the teenager.

....

do you mind is it a problem
take my word for it trust me; believe me

"Mr. Bermúdez, I want you to know that my mamá's home right now **crying her eyes out** over what this here hog done," Clarence said **in a monotone**. "This hog came to our place during the night and ruined our winter vegetable garden. All the cabbage, carrots, and most of the beets and greens are gone. They're ruined by this here **rooting** hog of yours."

"Sorry to hear that," Papá said.

"Mamá's crying 'cause we won't have much to eat now, just oranges and grapefruits. And we always get rashes when that's all we have to eat," Clarence said as he turned and headed toward the road.

If I had any joy at the return of Pánfilo, it **was short lived**. It didn't take long for Mamá to get the water and lime boiling again in the big black cauldron. My father asked Agustín to help him kill Pánfilo, but my brother said he couldn't because he had important business in town. Benny quickly volunteered to help. My mother told my father to quit wasting time and slaughter the hog himself. That is what he did while I watched from under the *guallín*.

Serapio and some of the neighbors helped my father scrape the mangy looking hair off of Pánfilo, and then they cut him up. My abuela made *chicharrones* while my mother cooked the head

....

crying her eyes out very upset
in a monotone without emotion
rooting digging
was short lived did not last long

and some other parts. About fifteen neighbor girls and women came to help make tamales, which everyone seemed to enjoy. My mother sent tamales, some ribs, and a shoulder to the Duncans.

Agustín said he was really going to miss my mother's cooking and he hoped it wouldn't be too long before he could be back home from the war to eat tamales again. But he never came back. He was sent to North Africa and was killed a few weeks after arriving. My father cried a lot over his death, and he drank a lot, too. I never saw my mother cry. And she never talked much after Agustín's death. In fact, she went months at a time without speaking to anyone. She spent most of her time cleaning things. She cleaned the house and everything in it. She cleaned the storage shed, the tractor shed, the corncrib, the privy, and anything else that had ever gotten dirty. However, she did not clean our little sleeping house. She never went in it, but she would stand at its doorway for long periods of time just looking in. Whenever I seemed concerned by **my mother's behavior**, my abuela would say, "**Have patience**, Paquito. Your mamá is very angry with God now. She doesn't talk to Him either."

My grandmother talked to God every day about Agustín. And she lit candles and also talked to the saints. She especially talked a lot to Our Lady of Guadalupe. Zulema told everybody

....

my mother's behavior the way my mother was acting
Have patience Be understanding

that she hated Japanese people but she mostly hated the Germans because they had killed her brother. Benny said he hated the United States of America for putting Agustín in the Army and sending him to the war and letting him get killed.

When my abuela heard him she said, "*¡Cállate la boca, huerco malo!* Just shut your mouth, bad boy!"

Soon after that, my abuela hung a framed picture of the flag of the United States on the wall. She put it between the photos of my brothers Agustín and Pancracio in their Army uniforms. Every time one of us youngsters came into the room where the pictures were hanging, Abuela would point her crooked finger at us and say, "Do you realize how lucky you are, child, to be living in the most wonderful country in the world? You need to think about this, and think about the sacrifice your brother made for this country and be proud you are an American!"

The winter that I lost Pánfilo and Agustín was a long time ago, but I've never forgotten the feelings of **anguish and despair** over giving up what was dear to me. Death was death, whether a pig or a brother. I struggled to **comprehend** it all. My family helped me **reconcile** the pig's death, and in time, I came to understand it. The death of my beloved brother could not be explained or accepted so easily.

....

anguish and despair sadness and pain
comprehend understand
reconcile accept

The Virgin and Doña Fidelfa

The only house on Garrapata Road that was colorfully painted was across the road from our farm. It was a little wooden house belonging to the widow Doña Fidelfa González. As far back as I can remember, the house was painted turquoise blue on the bottom half of the outside walls, and lilac on the top half. The trim around the windows and doors was painted pink. Scattered around Doña Fidelfa's backyard were several dozen coffee cans containing rosebushes. A large sign which read ROSES FOR SALE was nailed to the front of her house.

"I think Doña Fidelfa spends a lot of money for house paint," my mother said to me one day. "She sure keeps that old house of hers **freshly** painted."

It was true. My brothers usually painted it for her every year. And before that, my mother's brothers had painted it for her. Doña Fidelfa always paid my brothers for their work. One time

....

freshly newly

she even offered Mamá the leftover paint to use for our house but Mamá said no. It was tacky-looking paint and faded too quickly. But, of course, Mamá didn't tell that to Doña Fidelfa.

I came to know Doña Fidelfa well the summer I was seventeen. She had fallen and injured her hip. Because she had no one to care for her, Mamá sent me to stay with the poor old lady while she was **recuperating**. Being a tiny woman, she was no problem for me to handle. Besides keeping her clean, I cooked for her, washed and ironed her clothing, and cleaned her house. I also tended her rosebushes and sold a few of them for her from time to time. I always put her money away in the Bugler tobacco can that she kept in the kitchen cupboard.

Doña Fidelfa was friendly and kind to me and I grew fond of her. We got along very well, and I was content caring for her. We had **settled into the routine of** a quiet and uneventful summer, until Abelardo, Doña Fidelfa's nephew, unexpectedly arrived.

He came without anything except the clothes he was wearing, which were tattered and soiled. He looked **grizzled and road weary** and his obese body gave off a stench that made me recoil. He had a large mustache and an oily black beard. **His demeanor was surly.**

"Get me some coffee and something to eat, girl!" he ordered

....

recuperating healing; getting better
settled into the routine of been enjoying
grizzled and road weary old and tired
His demeanor was surly. He was very rude.

ten minutes after arriving. "And hurry."

He never said please, he never said thank you. He sat at the table and gulped down his food and belched, then gulped some more. When he was finished, he asked Doña Fidelfa for money.

"Why do you want money?" she asked.

"To buy new clothes so I won't be an embarrassment to you, dear aunt. Besides, how do you expect me to find work if I look like **a ragpicker**?"

Doña Fidelfa gave Abelardo ten dollars, telling him that was all she had. He left and came back that night without new clothing. However, he did have a new odor. It was whiskey.

And so it went with Abelardo. He wanted money daily from Doña Fidelfa, and she would give him a few dollars from time to time. He slept until noon and went into town every night. And he never got a job.

Doña Fidelfa's hip improved and she grew strong enough to hobble around her little house and, with my help, go outside to tend her roses. Although physically she seemed to be improving, something seemed wrong. She didn't appear as happy as before, and she didn't talk to me as much as was usual. She seemed to be **absorbed in thought** most of the day. Then, one night when we were alone in the kitchen, I noticed that she was talking

....

a ragpicker a homeless person

And so it went with Abelardo. Abelardo acted the same way everyday.

absorbed in thought thinking about something

apparently to no one, something she had not done before.

"Doña Fidelfa, did you say something to me?" I asked her.

"No, Zulema. I was not talking to you," she answered. "I was talking to myself. I said that I saw a light like a beautiful bright **halo** out in the back."

"Where was it?" I asked as I peered out through the screen door.

"Oh, it was out there by the privy."

I didn't see anything. "Well," I responded, "you've been telling me all summer that you see halos around the lights on the trucks. Maybe it was a truck light. You also said the moon has a halo."

"Well, the moon does have a halo. Especially when it is full. But the moon doesn't use the privy," she shook her finger at me and laughed. "Anyway, I'm sure I saw a light moving around out there."

I looked again, but couldn't see much in the dark, just the outlines of the privy, the storage shed, and the large fresno trees. I soon forgot about the light. Poor Doña Fidelfa continued mumbling to herself until she went to sleep.

Early the next morning, Doña Fidelfa asked me to accompany her out to the privy as usual. I sat down under the **crepe myrtle**

....

halo circle
crepe myrtle tree

to wait for her. Within a few seconds I heard her screaming, "*¡Santa María, Madre de Dios!* Zulema, come quickly!"

I jerked open the privy door and saw Doña Fidelfa on her knees with her underpants down around her ankles. I quickly stepped inside and closed the privy door. Doña Fidelfa remained kneeling with her eyes closed and her hands **in a posture of prayer**.

"What is it, Doña Fidelfa? Tell me."

She opened her eyes and said. "It's the Virgin, our Blessed Lady! Look! On the privy door! *¡Ay! ¡Madre Santa!*"

There was sufficient light coming through the cracks between the wall boards that I could see on the door what the woman was pointing to. There were blobs, and streaks, and **dribbles** of colors, mostly turquoise blue, pink, and lilac.

"There! Do you see the Virgin?" Doña Fidelfa asked.

"I don't see anything!" I responded.

I helped Doña Fidelfa get to her feet and pull up her underwear. I opened the privy door all the way until it stopped against the outside wall.

"Come on out, Doña Fidelfa. Let's look at the door from out here where we can see it better," I said as I helped her out of the privy.

....

¡Santa María, Madre de Dios! Saint María, Mother of God! (in Spanish)

in a posture of prayer joined together

dribbles dots, specks

We stood looking at the door.

"Move back a little bit, Zulema, and you can see her better."

I stepped back and looked at the **jumble** of colors again.

"Look," Doña Fidelfa instructed me. "Here is her head and her crown. See? And here is her halo." Her hand moved across the door. "And she has on a blue cape and a lilac gown. And see the little stars all over her cape?"

I peered at the door. "Tell me again where her head is," I said.

"There! Oh, Zulema, don't you see her?"

I must admit that I didn't see the Blessed Virgin as clearly as Doña Fidelfa did, but a person with a lot of imagination could probably **conjure up** the image of a woman in a gown and cape.

"Hurry, Zulema. Run get your mamá and the rest of your family," the excited woman said.

I obeyed and in about an hour there must have been a dozen people **assembled** around Doña Fidelfa's privy. Abelardo had been awakened by the noise and he came out to investigate. By evening he was giving guided tours to the groups of people that were coming to see the image of the Virgin.

The next day, Abelardo arose early and went to the storage shed where the paint was kept. He made a sign and nailed it to the front of the house. His sign said SEE THE BLESSED VIRGIN—DONATION 25¢. Next he removed the door from

....

jumble mix

conjure up see

assembled gathered

the privy and leaned it against the wall of the backside of the house. He then placed an old chair next to the privy door for Doña Fidelfa to sit in. He put a coffee can under the chair to hold the donations. After I had hung an old **drape over the gaping** doorway of the privy, Abelardo ordered me to arrange the cans of rosebushes all around the lower part of the privy door to help make it look "more **sacred**." Doña Fidelfa was now in business and it was thriving. She did very little but sit in her chair and collect the donations. Abelardo supervised the visitors and answered their questions. He seemed to know every inch of the Blessed Virgin, even down to her sandaled foot that he said was resting on a golden orb.

"Look carefully. Here is her head and her crown. Do you see her shining halo? Look at her beautiful star-covered cape," he would say as he ran his fat hand up and down the door.

About Doña Fidelfa he would say, "Yes, my tía is a very **humble and pious** woman, and a very poor woman. Is it not wonderful that our Blessed Virgin chose to visit my dear aunt who was confined to her bed, suffering greatly from her **infirmities**? And now she is cured."

Soon the story of the Virgin spread throughout South Texas. People came in wagons pulled by horses and mules. Some walked. Others came in farm trucks that brought dozens

....

drape over the gaping curtain over the open
sacred holy
humble and pious simple and religious
infirmities injuries

of people at one time. They came from distant towns and they came from local farms to look at the privy door. Many prayed for miracles. They donated nickels, dimes, and quarters to see the image. Some came more than once. Several refused to give donations because they claimed they could see nothing but spots where someone had cleaned a paintbrush. A reporter from a San Antonio newspaper came and interviewed Doña Fidelfa. The published article **no doubt** helped business because there was an increase in visitors for a while. Someone asked our priest to come look at the Virgin, but he refused. He said it was a fake and that the Blessed Virgin would never reveal herself in a privy. I heard he really got angry about it.

When school started in the fall, I had to return to my own home. Doña Fidelfa had recuperated by that time from her injury. I guess she must have given Abelardo some of her money because he bought new clothes. People continued to come to see the Virgin for several months after school started. Doña Fidelfa's coffee can under her chair filled up with coins time and time again. By Christmas the visitors had **dwindled** down to one or two a week. That was good, because some days were too chilly for Doña Fidelfa to sit outside and collect the money. It was at this time that Abelardo disappeared. I learned about it from

no doubt definitely, certainly
dwindled gone

Doña Fidelfa. One day I saw her tending her rosebushes, so I went over to visit with her. She told me Abelardo went to town one evening and never came back.

"Did he take his new clothes?" I asked.

"Oh, yes," she said. "And he took the privy door and the coffee can from under my chair."

I gasped, but I really wasn't surprised. I always supposed he was dishonest. "I'm sorry he stole all of your money."

"Oh no, Zulema, my dear. He took very little of it."

"What do you mean?" I was puzzled.

"Pick up that rosebush there." She pointed to one of the bushes planted in a coffee can.

I struggled to pick it up. It was heavy.

"Try lifting any of them," she said as she chuckled.

I tried another and another but they were as heavy as the first.

"Doña Fidelfa, **you didn't**?" I cried out.

"Oh yes. I did. I've known Abelardo all his life, and I've never trusted him. There is no way I would ever let him steal my money!"

....

you didn't you tricked him

BEFORE YOU MOVE ON...

1. **Comparisons** Reread pages 96–98. Compare Paco's feelings about the deaths of Pánfilo and Agustín.

2. **Inference** In "The Virgin and Doña Fidelfa," Doña Fidelfa sees a light in the privy the night before the image of the Virgin appears on the door. Is there a connection between these two events?

III

The Zambrano Family

A Reluctant Scholar

Texas **had a mandatory school attendance law** when I was a child in the 1930s and 40s. However, in my case, my mother chose to ignore this **mandate**. My two older brothers, Víctor and Mariano, got on the school bus every weekday morning and made the five-mile trip to El Tule. They were four and five years older than I, and they seemed to enjoy going to school. I couldn't imagine that at any age I would ever enjoy it. I **had a feeling of dread** when I thought of getting on that big bus and going into a town of people and places that I had never seen before.

After I had turned six years old, Víctor would from time to time arrive home from school and announce, "Mamá, the principal told me to tell you that Teo needs to come to school."

"Oh no, he doesn't," my mother would answer and shake her head slowly.

"But, Mamá, Teo turned six years old a long time ago.

....

had a mandatory school attendance law required all children
to go to school starting at six years old

mandate law, rule

had a feeling of dread felt miserable

111

Children start school at six," Víctor would remind her.

And Mamá would slowly shake her head and give her usual response. "My little Teódulo is old enough, but he is not tall enough to go to school."

If I were near her, she would pat me on top of my head as she spoke of my **stature**. Mamá seemed to relate school readiness to the size of a child, not the chronological age, as did the state of Texas. It was true that I was smaller than many boys my age. My grandmother said it was because I was **a premature** baby, and at birth I didn't weigh as much as a five-pound sack of roasted coffee beans. I was born at home and my grandmother calculated my weight by holding me in one hand and the sack of coffee beans in the other.

And so I stayed away from school until shortly before my ninth birthday. It was late November and already the eleventh week of the new school year when Víctor arrived home from school with a message from the principal.

"Mamá, the school **authorities** are going to come and get Teo and take him to school if you don't send him tomorrow."

I stopped eating my peanut butter taco and looked up at my tall handsome brother. He was standing behind my mother who was seated across from me at the kitchen table. Víctor's message

....

stature height, size
a premature an early
authorities officials

jolted me. I did not want authorities to come for me. I looked over at my mother expecting to see her head beginning to shake. But her head didn't move. She stopped cleaning the pinto beans that were spread before her on the table. She wiped her face with her greasy blue apron. Then she looked at me and smiled as she said, "I think he's big enough to go."

I couldn't believe she had said that. **My heart sank.** I must have had a horrible look on my face because Víctor walked over to me and patted me on my shoulder.

"Don't worry, Teo. It's not all that bad. And I'll stay with you in your classroom for a while tomorrow."

"Hey! No one stayed in class with me," said Mariano, who had been listening to all of this from the next room. "I had to go to first grade all by myself." Mariano quickly walked past me and grabbed the remainder of my taco from the table and popped it into his mouth.

Mamá ignored him and said, "Víctor, if you want to stay with Teo tomorrow, perhaps you should for a little while."

It seemed that I was **destined to** go to school. My **anxiety level** began to grow. I kept thinking of the bad things I had heard about school. My main concern was the fact that I did not understand English. Spanish was my sole language. The only

....

jolted surprised, shocked
My heart sank. I was very sad.
destined to supposed to
anxiety level nervousness

time I heard English was when Víctor and Mariano spoke it to keep me from knowing what they were saying. They had learned English at school. They said the students got into trouble with the teachers if they spoke Spanish.

I thought that Mamá would **change her mind about me going** to school, but she didn't. The next morning she got me out of bed early, and I got dressed in my newest shirt and my brown twill pants that Mamá had starched and ironed until they glistened. My only shoes were ill fitting, **hand-me-down** brown Oxfords that were gray from wear.

"Too bad we don't have any shoe polish," Mamá said to herself as she made bean tacos for me and my brothers to take to school for our lunches. "Teo, I'm going to let you take your lunch in this new paper bag," she said.

She wrapped my tacos in a piece of well-used butcher paper and carefully placed them in the small brown bag. "But please take good care of this bag and be sure to fold it nice and bring it home. Do not leave it at school. Do you understand?"

I knew how **precious** paper bags were. We had to reuse them many times. When we were out of bags, my brothers had to take their tacos to school in lard cans like the girls did. They didn't like that. I looked at the tattered bag that held my brothers' tacos

....

change her mind about me going decide that I should not go
hand-me-down used
precious special, rare

and I promised my mother that I'd take good care of the new bag. Then I, with my brothers, made my first walk down Garrapata Road to the bus stop. My mother watched us from the door. I think she was crying.

The trip to El Tule **was a blur**. Víctor and Mariano stuffed me between them in the seat they shared. The bus rattled and shook as it stopped and started along its route picking up farm and ranch children. I couldn't see much, but I could faintly hear what I thought to be children laughing and singing. I **paid them no attention** as my mind was on the horrible things that awaited me at El Tule Elementary School.

After we exited the bus at the school, Mariano left Víctor and me without even saying good-bye. Víctor and I went to the principal's office, where Víctor gave the secretary the information that was needed for **my enrollment**. I comprehended none of it. I stood as close to Víctor as I could and clung tightly to the brown paper bag which held my tacos.

Then Víctor said he would take me to my classroom. My stomach was beginning to feel jumpy as we walked down a wide hall with a very tall ceiling. My stomach began faintly cramping. Perhaps I was getting sick and someone would have to take me home. That would be nice.

....

was a blur is not something that I remember because I was so nervous

paid them no attention ignored them

my enrollment me to sign up for school

The cramps **subsided** by the time we walked into the first grade classroom. The room was full of little tables and chairs, and boys and girls were noisily beginning to take their seats. Víctor said a few things to a young woman in a purple dress who was standing just inside the doorway. The woman was small and frail looking. She had blond curly hair and red stuff on her cheeks and mouth. She pointed to an empty chair at a table at the back of the room where three children were already seated. Víctor had me sit down. A bell rang and I jumped and **made a loud gasping sound**. A few students who were watching me laughed. Then the young woman in the purple dress said something in English to Víctor. He turned back to me and put his hand on my shoulder.

"I'm sorry, little brother, Miss McClean says I can't stay with you. It's **against school rules**. We have to do what Miss McClean says. She's your teacher."

I grabbed Víctor's arm and held it tightly.

Víctor **winced**. "Teo, please. I have to go."

I continued to hold on.

"You'll be fine. And I'll meet you at the front door as soon as school is out. Just wait for me there," Víctor said.

I let go of his arm and watched him hurry out. I began to cry.

....

subsided went away
made a loud gasping sound got scared
against school rules not allowed
winced felt bad; frowned

Not too loudly, just as quietly as I could. Some of the students looked at me and laughed. But the little girl sitting across the table from me began to cry also. She was bawling loudly. I put my head down on the table and covered my ears with my hands. The girl quit making her noise. I kept my head down.

Miss McClean came over to my table and gently shook me. "What's your name?" she said as she looked at me without smiling.

I sat up and, not understanding, didn't respond. So she repeated her question louder. I still didn't understand. The boy to my left repeated to me in Spanish what Miss McClean had asked.

I looked up at her and quietly said, "Teódulo Zambrano."

"Oh, my goodness," she replied. "I can't say that or even remember it. I'll just have to give you a better name."

She wrote something down on a little lined card and looked at me again. "Okay, we'll call you Teddy. Now you remember your new name. Okay. Teddy?"

The boy to my left, who was **undoubtedly becoming my interpreter**, told me about my new name. This didn't make me happy. My name wasn't Teddy. That was an ugly name.

"Our teacher is new here. She can't speak Spanish," my interpreter said. "My name is Melquiades but she calls me

....

undoubtedly becoming my interpreter repeating what the teacher said in Spanish so that I could understand

Melvin, and I like it okay."

Just then Miss McClean made an announcement and passed out books to each student. She had a **stern** look on her face, but I noticed that she was pretty. And I was especially fascinated with her sparkling blue eyes.

I asked Melquiades what she had said.

He answered, "It's time for our reading groups."

"What does that mean?" I asked.

"We take turns reading about the little American children and their dog and cat."

I opened my reading book and looked at the pictures. They were pretty to look at, but there was no way I could read anything about these pictures.

I noticed that Miss McClean was passing out small American flags. She placed one of the flags in front of me. I was delighted that she had given me something, especially something that I had never had before. I picked it up and carefully inspected it. There was a tiny cloth flag attached to a wooden **dowel** that had a gold pointed thing at one end. The other end of the dowel was placed in a wooden **pedestal**.

"Teddy, you have the flag. You start the reading for our table," said Melquiades.

....

stern serious
dowel stick
pedestal base, holder

I placed the flag back on the table in front of me and opened the reading book.

"Hurry, Teddy. Start on page five," said Melquiades.

My other two tablemates had their books open and were staring at me. The girl across from me had stopped crying, but was now **emitting** an occasional sob. Her face looked swollen and red.

Melquiades had to show me the page. I looked at the page that had a colorful picture of children playing in a nice yard with their dog and cat and a little red wagon. I couldn't read anything, so I just sat there looking at the pictures.

Miss McClean walked over to me and said, "Sorry, Teddy. I guess it's too soon for you. We'll let Melvin start this group."

Miss McClean picked up the little flag by its dowel just as I grabbed its pedestal and yanked. She must have pulled it toward her because the dowel came loose from the pedestal and the pointed end struck her in her chest. I was horrified. She **grimaced** but otherwise ignored what happened and placed the dowel back into the pedestal. She set the flag in front of Melquiades. I was hurt that she took the flag away from me. Didn't she give it to me? Wasn't it supposed to be mine? It was difficult to understand Miss McClean's actions.

....

emitting letting out
grimaced was not happy; was annoyed

Melquiades read for a while, then he picked up the flag and placed it in front of the girl across from me. She read and then passed the flag to the boy to my right. It was while he was **laboriously** reading that I realized I needed to **relieve my bladder**. I didn't know what to do and I was afraid to say anything to Miss McClean who was walking around the room **monitoring** the reading groups. So I held it and held it.

Finally, I whispered to Melquiades, "I have to make pee."

"You have to tell Miss McClean," he said.

"She won't understand me," I replied.

"Just say 'May I be excused?'" said Melquiades.

That was English! I couldn't say any English. I held back my tears but I couldn't hold back my pee. I felt the warm urine spread across the front of my pants and then down through my legs. My tablemates continued reading and passing the American flag around the table. I wanted to get up and run out, but I didn't know where I would go. Just as I was planning my escape, Miss McClean made an announcement and everyone stopped reading and placed their books in a stack in the middle of the table. The little flags were placed on top of the stacks.

"Time for recess," said Melquiades.

The children made a line at the door. The bell rang and the

---

laboriously slowly
relieve my bladder go to the bathroom
monitoring observing, watching

line moved out into the hall. I walked slowly holding my tacos in the paper bag in front of my wet pants. I hoped no one would notice the wet spot. Once outside I found a place to hide between the building and some large bushes. I ate my tacos while standing with my legs wide apart so the air would help dry my clothing. It never occurred to me that I should have saved a taco for lunch. I'm not sure I knew the difference between recess and lunch anyway.

When the bell rang, I saw my classmates going back into the building so I followed them. My pants were still wet, but I didn't really care. I just wanted the day to be over.

Next, Miss McClean passed out green wooden blocks and cards with numbers printed on them. We had to match the numbers with the same amount of blocks. We worked as a group and I let my tablemates do all the work. I didn't know how to read numbers. By watching the other students, I began to **catch on** and by the time the bell rang again, I was almost enjoying myself.

Miss McClean said something to the class.

"Time for lunch," said Melquiades.

"Can I stay with you?" I asked, knowing that I'd be alone because Víctor and Mariano had lunch at a different time.

"I have to go home to eat. I just live down the street," said

....

catch on understand what I was supposed to do

Melquiades and he quickly left.

I spent the lunch hour standing between the building and the bushes and thinking about my tacos that I had already eaten. I was glad when it was time to go back into the classroom, as I was ready to sit down. My pants were dry now, so I felt more at ease.

Melquiades came back from lunch with ***carne guisada*** juice drying on his chin. While I was looking hungrily at Melquiades's chin, a tall lady in a dark-blue dress came into the classroom. Miss McClean made an announcement and the tall lady began going from table to table running the pointed end of a rat-tail comb through each child's hair. She bent over each head, wrinkled her nose, and peered intently as she **gingerly raked** through the hair.

I was puzzled so I looked at Melquiades.

"She's the school nurse," he said. "She's just looking for *piojos*."

Lice! I had heard of lice, but no one in my family had ever had them. My mother would have never **allowed that**. The nurse came over to my table. She sniffed several times as she ran the comb's tail through my hair. Perhaps she smelled the dried urine. Perhaps it was just the Four Roses brilliantine that Víctor had put on my hair.

After the nurse had examined all the children, she selected

....

carne guisada beef stew (in Spanish)
gingerly raked carefully combed
allowed that let that happen

several and took them out of class. Melquiades was one of them. My interpreter did not return for the rest of the school day.

Next, Miss McClean passed out cigar boxes filled with pieces of Crayola crayons and pictures for us to color. I was glad because here was an activity that I was good at and that I enjoyed. I could be very successful with coloring my picture, which was a clown holding a hoop for a dog to jump through. Just as I was preparing to select some crayons from the box, Miss McClean approached me.

"While the children are doing art work, you come sit with me at my desk so I can help you with reading. **What a shame** that you are so very far behind."

She motioned for me to come and sit down beside her.

"And everyday during art time, I'll work with you on reading. Do you understand, Teddy?"

No. All I understood was that she had now taken back the picture of the clown with his dog and I had to look at the flash cards with pictures and words that Miss McClean held up to me.

"Look, Teddy. What is this?" she asked as she held up a card.

"*Gato*," I said, looking at a picture of a fluffy gray cat.

"No, Teddy," she said as she **waggled her delicate white index** finger at me. "It's not a *gato*. It's a cat. See? CAT. Look

....

What a shame It is not good
waggled her delicate white index pointed her

at the word."

"*Gato*," I repeated. She was wrong. It was a *gato*. I knew a *gato* when I saw a *gato*.

We continued like this for what seemed a very long time. Every animal and object she showed me on her cards were familiar to me. I knew the names, but none of them were what she wanted to hear. She began to **appear frustrated**, so I was glad when she sent me back to my table where I sat doing nothing for the rest of the school day.

When the dismissal bell rang, I went directly to the front of the building to find Víctor and Mariano. I waited a while. Then I remembered my paper bag. I hurried back down the hall and stopped just outside my classroom door. I quietly peeked inside to see if anyone was there. Miss McClean was there alone. She was sitting at her desk, slumped over with her face in her hands. I could faintly hear her weeping. Her frail body was **slightly heaving** with each sob. I quietly **tiptoed** into the room and over to the shelf where I had hidden my folded bag under a big book. Miss McClean saw me and motioned for me to come over to her. Cautiously I approached her. She smiled and put the palm of her hand against my cheek. Her sparkling blue eyes were full of tears. In understandable but strangely pronounced Spanish, she said,

....

appear frustrated get discouraged; get upset that I was not understanding

slightly heaving moving

tiptoed walked

"Please come back tomorrow, Teddy."

I did return the next day, and every school day for the **remainder** of that school year. I learned to read the stories about the American children and their dog and cat. I learned a lot about the world in that classroom. I think Miss McClean did too. But she never learned to say my name.

....

remainder rest

The Battle of the Blackbirds

Baseball was an important part of my life growing up on Garrapata Road. Most of the farm boys in our neighborhood spent a lot of their free time playing this game. A few of the girls played, too, like Nilda Paloma who looked like a boy and acted like a boy and played baseball like a boy. But nobody really liked her or wanted to play with her. My brother, Víctor, had gotten a team together, and I wanted so badly to play with him and the older guys.

"I'm sorry, Teódulo, you're too young. You need to wait a couple of years," Víctor said as he smiled at me.

I admired his tall, **lanky** body and wished I could be like him. Or at least like my brother Mariano who was a little older than me, but a lot bigger. I envied Mariano because he was allowed to play on Víctor's team.

----

lanky thin

Víctor's team was made up of young men from the neighboring farms, except for the shortstop, Cookie Zambrano, who was our cousin. He lived in town, and he thought he was better than we were because his family had a flush toilet in their house. He said our privy was full of spiders and smelled bad and he didn't like to use it. We really didn't like Cookie very much anyway, but he was our *primo* and a good baseball player.

It was Cookie that helped my dreams of playing baseball on Víctor's team **come true**. He announced to Víctor at practice one evening in late spring that he wasn't going to be playing with Víctor's team anymore.

"I've been asked to play with the El Tule Cuervos. They have new uniforms," Cookie said.

"Do what you have to do," Víctor said. He crushed a clod of dirt with a spike of his baseball shoe.

"Well, this team of yours doesn't play any teams **of any importance**, just a bunch of ragged farm and ranch teams," Cookie added as he pulled his Bugler tobacco out of his pocket and rolled a cigarette.

"I said, do what you have to do," Víctor replied.

"And just look at this playing field. An old dirt landing strip in the middle of a pasture. Not good for anything. And you

....

primo cousin (in Spanish)
come true happen; become reality
of any importance that are good

don't have uniforms. You don't even have a name for your team."
Cookie turned on his heel. "This team is **just a joke**."

"That's right, Cookie. You go on and play for the town team.
We can do without you," Víctor said as he motioned for Mariano
and me to go on to the house.

Oh, good, I thought. I'm glad Cookie's going to play with
those **smart-alecky** Cuervos from town. And what an ugly name
for a team. Cuervos. Crows! Well, maybe I can play on Víctor's
team now.

When Víctor came into the house, Mariano asked the
question that I was just dying to ask, but was afraid to.

"I guess Teódulo will have to take Cookie's place on the team
now that we're down to eight players. Right, Víctor?"

"I don't know. He's only thirteen," my big brother answered
without looking at me.

"And we've played **a man short** before."

"Well, we can always ask Nilda Paloma. In fact she'll
probably be over here today begging to play with us. She did that
the last time we were missing a man," Mariano said. He turned
his head so Víctor couldn't see he was smiling.

"And that's just the problem. She's not a man. People don't
approve of her playing baseball. Girls aren't supposed to play

....

just a joke terrible
smart-alecky mean
a man short without all of the players

baseball, especially not with men," replied Víctor.

"All she needs is a husband," Mariano replied. "He'd **keep her in her place**."

Víctor slightly smiled, but he didn't say anything. Deep down he knew that Nilda was a good athlete and she could play baseball. He wished she wasn't a female.

Mariano opened an RC Cola and took a big swallow. He offered the bottle to Víctor and continued talking. "Well, we have a game on Sunday with the Gatos. Are we going to play a man short?"

"No. Teo can play. I'll put him in right field."

I was thrilled. My brother said that I could play. How important I felt! The other boys my age would come to watch the games and see that I was playing with the older guys. They would all be **envious** of me. And maybe my Papá would go to Reynosa and buy me a new glove to replace Mariano's **old beat-up secondhand one** that I was using.

On Friday night our plan for a game on Sunday was changed when the Gatos' pitcher, Lucas Lozano, came by our house to tell Víctor that the Enriquez brothers had gone to Petronila because their grandmother had died. The four Enriquez brothers, their uncle, and two cousins played for the Gatos, and with them gone,

....

keep her in her place tell her how to behave
envious jealous
old beat-up secondhand one old and worn glove

they had no team. We were disappointed, especially me. I was really looking forward to playing on Sunday, even though my father had refused to buy me a new glove.

On Saturday morning Cookie came by our house just to find out how we were going to **manage** our game against the Gatos without him. He seemed a little disappointed when he learned our Sunday game had been canceled.

On Saturday afternoon Cookie returned to our place with Braulio Jiménez, the Cuervos' manager and **ace** pitcher.

"Listen, Víctor. What about your team playing our team tomorrow," Braulio said. "The Cuervos don't have a game scheduled, and it would give your team some good practice to play against **a first-class** team."

"Yes, sir. A first-class team," said Cookie. He smiled and tried to spit between his teeth but the spittle ran down his chin as usual.

I looked at Cookie, then at Braulio. I didn't know which one was the ugliest: Cookie, with his oily mustache and skinny neck that showed his big jumpy Adam's apple, or Braulio, fat, sweaty, and sour looking.

Víctor chuckled and said, "Sure. We'll be glad to play you. Only you have to come over here to our field."

"Well, I don't know," said Braulio as he scratched his head

---

manage play

ace best

a first-class an excellent

130

with his dirty fingernails.

"It's here, or not at all," replied Víctor.

"Well, okay. But you have to provide two new balls for the game. And not any of those cheap Rabbit brand balls from Mexico," Braulio said and **smirked** at Víctor.

"We will have new baseballs," said Víctor and he kicked a dirt clod with his foot causing a cloud of dust to rise.

"And your team needs a real name, too. 'Víctor's Team' isn't a name," added Cookie.

"We have a name," replied Víctor. "It's the Grackles."

Oh, no! I nearly choked. Not grackles, those dirty, noisy blackbirds. I hated those stinking birds! Why did he say that was our name? Why couldn't we just be the Dodgers, or Tigers, or Giants?

For the rest of the day I didn't have much time to think about our team being called Grackles, as Víctor gave me his and Mariano's chores to do so they could take care of baseball business. They had to go **take up a collection** from all of the team members so Víctor would have enough money to buy some American-made baseballs. Mariano collected some of our empty soda pop bottles so he could get the deposit money back from the grocery store.

....

smirked smiled meanly

take up a collection ask for money; get donations

After my chores were done, I went with Papá to buy bottles of RC Cola and Delaware Punch that Mamá would **ice down** in a big round tub and sell at the game. Papá also bought some Orange Crush, but those were special for Mamá to drink. I wanted a big ginger cookie shaped like a pig, so Papá bought one for me and one for Mamá. But Papá ate hers before we got home.

The next morning Víctor woke me up at daylight. We needed to go to the landing strip and mark off the playing field. I grabbed a few long nails and the hammer. Next I gathered up string, the **base spikes**, and lime and threw them in the back of the pickup truck. Mariano had already put the canvas bases in the truck and was in the storage shed looking for the rubber home plate.

"I've got the plate over here," Víctor said as he held up the plate that was almost ripped into two pieces.

"What'll we do? It's too late to buy a new plate, and we don't have any money anyway, not after paying for those darn fancy balls," said Mariano.

"We'll use this plate and hope it will stay together," responded Víctor as he gently laid the home plate in the back of the truck.

We worked on the field most of the morning, stretching string along the baselines, then pouring from a small coffee can, the white chalky lime along the string. Víctor constructed the

....

ice down keep cold
base spikes nails for the bases

pitcher's mound, smoothing and packing the dirt and watering it down until it looked and felt just right to him.

We had everything ready by the time the spectators in their cars, pickups, and farm trucks began arriving for the game. They parked in long lines along the sides of the diamond. Many of the pickup trucks backed in to allow people to watch the game while sitting on the **tailgates**. The Cuervos showed up in their cars and pickups, honking and yelling like crazy people. They had on beautiful new uniforms. Our team wore nothing that looked like a uniform. Most of us wore jeans or khaki pants and tee shirts. Víctor and Mariano each wore an old ragged baseball shirt that had belonged to Papá. Our caps were a variety of colors and conditions. Víctor and Dizzy Durán were our only team members that owned baseball shoes. The rest of us wore our black, high-top Converse canvas shoes. Those ugly ones.

When the Cuervo players saw us they hooted and laughed and whistled and yelled at us.

"Look at the *traperos*, the ragpickers. What beautiful uniforms those Grackles have on."

The Cuervo players also used **foul** language and called us nasty names. Víctor told us to ignore them but I could tell he was angry because the muscles in front of his ears moved up and

....

tailgates backs of the trucks
foul bad

down. My father didn't like what the Cuervos said because there were women and children at the game. My grandmother was even there sitting on the tailgate of Víctor's pickup, right where she sat every Sunday afternoon that Víctor's team played.

"Remember," Papá told us, "uniforms don't make a team play any better or any worse. And you don't need fancy uniforms to beat the Cuervos."

Well, the game started and I was really nervous. Those darn Cuervos scored three runs before the beginning of the third inning. Víctor kept telling us to calm down, but it was really hard. The Cuervos had a few hits into right field. I caught one **high fly** and had to run after the others.

We finally had some good luck when in the seventh inning Yoyo Durán and Víctor each scored a run for us. And in the eighth, Chuy Chávez and Dizzy scored two more. Now we were one run ahead with one inning to go. The Cuervos came up to bat in the top of the ninth. Their first two batters were thrown out at first. Just one more out and the game would be ours. Then José María Mondragón came up to bat. José María was the Cuervos' **powerhouse**. He was six feet two and weighed 300 pounds. It was said he could knock a baseball 350 feet without trying. He hit a high fly on his first swing. I saw that it was coming toward me.

....

high fly ball that went high into the air
powerhouse strongest player

I remembered the only rule Víctor taught me about catching fly balls. Catch them anyway you can. The sun was behind me and I could clearly see the ball coming. I saw it **arc** and start down, so I got under it. I **planted** my feet firmly on the ground, looked up, and stretched my arms high above my head with the glove wide open.

I wish I could say that I caught that ball and thus won the game. But I can't. I dropped the ball. I heard Mariano say, "Hustle, Teo, hustle." I picked up the ball and threw it to Chuy Chávez on second, but José María beat the throw. At least we held him on second base.

It would be up to Víctor to save the game for us and he did. Cookie came up to bat and Víctor struck him out, three strikes in a row. We had won! But that stupid José María Mondragón stayed standing on second base and Cookie continued to hold on to the bat at home plate like he was expecting another pitch.

None of the Cuervos moved or said anything. They looked so ridiculous just standing **motionless and mute**. We came running in off the field and the Cuervos finally came to the realization that they had lost the game to the Grackles, the *traperos*, the ragpickers. They began screaming at us and screaming at the umpire. Their language was ugly, foul, and

....

arc go up high
planted set, put
motionless and mute still and not speaking

despicable. José María Mondragón picked up the home plate and finished ripping it into two pieces with his huge hands. Braulio tore first base open with his pocketknife and scattered the straw stuffing over the field.

My father and some of the other men **intervened** and threatened to go get the sheriff if the Cuervos didn't leave. The Cuervos gathered up their equipment, but before they left, one of them took a bat and broke a headlight out of Víctor's pickup even while my grandmother was sitting on the tailgate. Víctor told me to stay near him until the Cuervos left.

"Well, we'll never play that **bunch of ruffians** again," Víctor said and shook his head. "We usually have lots of fun playing baseball."

Cookie stayed behind to talk to Víctor. "I'm sorry, *primo*," he said. "I didn't know those Cuervos were like that. I don't really want to play on their team, so I'll just come back to yours."

"Sorry, Cookie, we don't need you right now," Víctor replied as he put his hand on my shoulder. "But I'll let you know if we ever do."

....

intervened got involved;
tried to stop the Cuervos

bunch of ruffians rough
team

BEFORE YOU MOVE ON...

1. **Inference** Reread pages 124–125. Why does Miss McClean cry and ask Teódulo to come back to school?

2. **Conclusions** Reread pages 135–136. Why does Víctor let Teódulo on the team after they win but not Cookie?

IV

The Paloma Family

Crazy Rita

After my brother Zeke came home from the war, he announced to us that he planned to marry Rita Rincón. I was delighted to hear this because I thought that it would be like having another sister to help me with the work around the house, especially with my sister Juana spending so much time away from home. But my mother didn't seem very happy about Zeke's choice.

"Are you certain about this, son?" she had asked.

"Of course, Mamá. Please don't worry about it."

"It's just that she seems to be such a strange girl. And I don't like it that people call her Crazy Rita. Don't you feel that way, too, Nilda?" my mother had said without looking up from the shirt that she was **mending**.

Yes, I thought Rita was strange. And it was true that a lot of people said that she was a little crazy. I think Rita probably

....

mending sewing, fixing

deserved it, because I remember she did a lot of weird things, especially as a **youngster**. One September she supposedly spent three days in a chinaberry tree without coming down because she didn't want to go to school. I heard she only came down when she fell out of the tree so weak from hunger that she couldn't hold on any longer.

Another time she and her dog disappeared from home and the entire neighborhood went looking for her. Some of the men and boys took lanterns and searched all night for her because the Widow Rincón, **in a fit of desperation**, had offered a reward of fifty dollars to whomever found her missing daughter. Rita was found the next morning hiding in a thick growth of *nopal* cactus and *mezquite*. Someone reported that her clothing was hanging in shreds from her body. She had taken the sash from her dress and tied her dog's muzzle so he couldn't bark and reveal her hiding place. I think she had run away because one of her brothers had **slapped her around**.

In defense of Rita, I must say that as she grew older she seemed to calm down. She no longer was the topic of neighborhood gossip and I seldom saw her except at mass on Sundays. She had become a beautiful young woman, tall and slender with long black wavy hair. It was not difficult to

....

youngster child

in a fit of desperation ready to try anything

slapped her around hit her

understand why my brother was attracted to her.

When my father heard that Rita was to be his daughter-in-law, he didn't say much about it. He helped Zeke build a little one-room house out behind our house so the young couple would have their own place. Zeke furnished the house with a bed, a chair, a footlocker, and a chifforobe. Then my father accompanied Zeke to ask the Widow Rincón for **her daughter's hand in marriage**.

My father told Mamá and me that the visit wasn't very pleasant. According to my father, when he requested the Widow Rincón's permission for Zeke to marry her daughter, she **turned purple in the face**.

"Absolutely not! My precious daughter will never marry that good-for-nothing son of yours!" the Widow Rincón had screamed and shook her fat index finger at my father. "I would have to be out of my mind to let you take away the only daughter I have!" she said and beat her ample chest with her fist. "Just look around! Do you see my husband? No! I've been a widow for many years," she said and took a big breath for **her finale**. "Do you see my sons? No! They have left me and gone up north to work. Rita is all I have." Then she closed her eyes and pointed toward the door. "Get out of my house and don't come back!"

....

her daughter's hand in marriage permission to marry her daughter

turned purple in the face got extremely angry

her finale the end of her speech

My mother was very angry to hear this report from my father. She was proud of Zeke and very protective of him.

"Well, did you tell that horrible woman that our son is a very brave man? That he joined the Army and went to war to defend this country against Hitler? That my son is a hardworking man and can make a good living helping you with farming? Did you tell her that Zeke already has his own little house here on the farm, and that someday forty acres of this farm will be his? Well, husband, did you tell her that?"

My father was sitting at the kitchen table sharpening his pocketknife. "No, I said nothing. Zeke and I left her house as she demanded," my father said as he looked closely at the **whetstone**, spat on it, and continued with the sharpening. "But listen to this," he said. "Rita followed us outside and said it didn't matter what her mother thought. She wants to marry Zeke anyway, even without her mother's **blessing**."

In time Zeke and Rita were married. The Widow Rincón was so angry that she refused to attend the church ceremony or the wedding supper that my parents hosted in our backyard. Rita supposedly told Zeke that her mother had **disowned her** and had said she never wanted to see her again.

The day after the wedding was Sunday, and Zeke and Rita

....

whetstone sharpening stone
blessing permission
disowned her told her she was no longer part of the family

attended mass. But Rita did not return to our farm with my brother. I was somewhat disappointed and asked Zeke about her.

"She had some things to do at her mother's house. Don't worry, Nilda. I'll go get her later."

But Rita didn't come back with Zeke that day. I guess the Widow Rincón decided she wanted to see Rita again after all, because it was almost a week before Zeke brought Rita back. I could tell when she got out of the truck that she had been crying. She didn't seem to notice me and **went straight out** to the little house.

Sometime in the middle of the night something awakened me. I saw light coming from the window of the little house and I heard loud voices. I thought I could hear Rita crying.

For the next three nights the same thing happened. I wanted to ask Zeke what was going on in his house, but I was afraid it might embarrass him. However, my mother didn't hesitate to say something to him when he came in alone for breakfast.

"Son, was there a problem in your house during the night? I saw your lantern burning late and it was still burning early this morning."

Zeke added milk to his coffee and stirred in four teaspoons of sugar. "Mamá, I **don't know what to tell you**."

---

went straight out immediately went

don't know what to tell you do not know what the problem is

"I can see in your face something is wrong," my mother said as she laid her hand against Zeke's cheek. "Your eyes are **bloodshot** and your face is drawn. I insist you tell me about the problem."

"Rita says something is weird with her pillow. According to her, it keeps waking her up every night. She's very upset because she can't sleep at night," Zeke said in a hushed voice.

"Now, **pray** tell me how a pillow can wake her up," responded my mother as she pinched off a piece of sweet bread and popped it into her mouth.

Zeke sighed and kept his gaze on his coffee cup. "Rita says her pillow rises up off the bed. That's what wakes her up. She's too afraid to go back to sleep when that happens. She wants the lantern burning all night. It's hard for me to sleep."

"And when did this problem begin?" my mother asked, and I noted a somewhat **skeptical** tone to her voice.

"Rita says it only happens here. It never happened before she moved in with me," my brother replied as he quickly finished his coffee.

My mother's eyes narrowed. "I don't believe that about her pillow. Do you believe that, Nilda?" Mamá said.

"I don't know what to believe," I answered, "but I know

....

bloodshot red
pray please
skeptical doubtful

something is wrong, because I've heard Rita crying every night for the past four nights. I've also seen their lantern light every time I've looked out my window during the night."

"Well, I'm certainly going to talk to Rita," Mamá said and she rose and walked out the kitchen door and out to the little house.

In about half an hour my mother returned. I was still at the breakfast table, but Zeke had gone to join my father who had been out on his tractor since early morning.

"Nilda, tonight you need to get the sleeping mat from under your bed and take it out to the little house," my mother ordered. "I want you to sleep on the floor near Rita, and you find out if her pillow is rising up off the bed."

I wasn't sure if I really wanted to do that. Rita and Zeke said I was welcome to sleep on the floor if I wanted to. It might be interesting, I thought, because in all of my seventeen years, I had never heard of a pillow rising by itself off of the bed. I was a little **apprehensive**, but I knew that Zeke would protect me, or at least I thought he would. I just didn't know **from what**.

Rita was already in bed when I arrived after dark with my sleeping mat. I quickly made me a bed and lay down. Zeke came in and **snuffed** out the lantern, which put us into a darkness that

....

apprehensive afraid, fearful
from what what I needed protection from
snuffed put

made me feel **jittery**. Somehow I finally went to sleep.

Sometime later, I heard Rita whimpering. I sat up quickly and reached out in the darkness toward her. Even though I couldn't see well in the darkened room, I could sense that she was struggling with her pillow.

"Zeke! Hurry! Light the lantern," I called out.

Zeke was already **fumbling with** the matches. When the lantern was lit, we could see Rita sitting up, facing the head of the bed, and clutching her pillow to her body.

"See! It's happened again," she **blubbered**. She covered her face with her hands and sobbed.

"What happened, Rita?" I asked.

She stopped crying. "It awakened me again. The pillow was up in the air, hovering above the bed with my head still on it." She looked at me with wide unblinking eyes. "This is driving me absolutely crazy, Nilda. What can I do?" She began to cry again.

I put my arms around her and felt that her body was trembling. She was sobbing so loudly that I decided not to say anything.

Zeke cried out, "My God. Rita! I've got to get some sleep! Just sleep without your darned pillow!" He turned over in the bed and pulled the covers over his head.

....

jittery nervous
fumbling with trying to light
blubbered cried

"I'm so sorry," Rita said. "But please don't put out the lantern. I'm afraid."

So the three of us slept the rest of the night with the lantern burning. I guess the pillow stayed on the bed. At least Rita didn't awaken me again.

The next morning I told my mother what had happened. She told the story to my aunts and also to my grandmother who lived a mile from us down Garrapata Road. That afternoon my grandmother arrived at our house bringing with her, not only two of my aunts, but Doña Migdalia Tovar, the unofficial **trouble shooter** of the neighborhood. My mother served the usual cups of coffee and pieces of sweet bread to the women.

"So Rita's pillow is rising from her bed," said Doña Migdalia as she sucked coffee into her toothless mouth.

Then she looked across the kitchen table at my mother and chuckled. Doña Migdalia's mass of tangled white hair gave her a look of wildness. For years I had feared her. I'm not sure why. Probably because all of my friends did.

"Something is happening to Rita's pillow. Isn't that right, Nilda?" my mother said.

I didn't know how to answer her question. Something was happening, but I wasn't sure if it had anything to do with

---

trouble shooter problem solver

Rita's pillow.

"Nilda! Isn't that right?" my mother repeated.

"Yes, something is happening," I replied.

Doña Migdalia threw back her head and gulped down the last bit of her coffee. "I had better take a look at that pillow," she said.

My mother and I took my aunts, my grandmother, and Doña Migdalia out to the little house. An exhausted Rita was lying asleep on my mat on the floor. She had no pillow under her head. She awakened when the six of us crowded into the room.

"Where is this strange pillow, girl?" Doña Migdalia asked Rita.

Poor alarmed Rita sat up and stared with large unblinking eyes. She pointed at the pillow that lay on her side of the bed. Doña Migdalia moved about rubbing her palms across the pillow, the bed, the footlocker, the chair, and even across Rita's body. Then she stood still with her eyes closed and her arms outstretched in front of her. No one moved or said anything for about a minute.

Doña Migdalia lowered her arms and said in a calm voice, "Well, it is very obvious. It can only be one thing."

"What is it? What is it?" my mother and grandmother asked **in unison**.

....

in unison at the same time

Doña Migdalia continued, "There is a treasure buried under this little house. Rita is sensitive enough to detect it. She has a gift from God which helps her find treasures wherever they are **concealed**."

"And what should be done?" my grandmother asked and shook her head in **apparent consternation**.

"Your grandson must tear down this little house and dig up the treasure, of course," answered Doña Migdalia. "Otherwise, he and Rita will never get a night's rest."

When Zeke came in from the fields that evening and heard about Migdalia and her message, he became very angry. He and Rita had a long private talk in their little house. It wasn't totally private as I could hear a lot of what they said because they were talking rather loudly.

Finally, just before dark, I saw Zeke and Rita loading things in the back of Zeke's truck. Later Zeke came to the kitchen door. My mother, father, and I were eating supper. Zeke cleared his throat several times and then said that he and Rita were going to go stay with the Widow Rincón. It would be only for a short while, just until they could get some rest. Perhaps everything would be all right when they returned. He promised that he would be back home soon.

....

concealed hidden
apparent consternation surprise

The Widow Rincón undoubtedly was so happy to have her daughter back home that she gladly allowed my brother to stay, too. Zeke's visit wasn't temporary as he had promised. He and Rita never returned to the little house on our farm because a few months after they moved in with the Widow Rincón, the old woman died. She had been a somewhat wealthy woman. She left all her money and her six-thousand-acre **irrigated** farm to her beloved Rita. Today, my brother is one of the most **affluent** farmers in this area, and my mother is very pleased to have Crazy Rita for a daughter-in-law.

....

irrigated modern
affluent wealthy

BEFORE YOU MOVE ON...

1. **Inference** Reread pages 143–145. What does Rita complain about? What is really upsetting her?

2. **Plot** Reread pages 149–150. What changes after Rita inherits the Widow Rincón's money and farm?

The Prisoner

My brother, Roberto, was a prisoner of the Japanese for most of the Second World War. He was **captured** during the fall of Bataan and we never knew anything for certain about him until the war was over.

"I'll believe he's alive when I see him walk through the door," Mamá had said the day we received the **telegram** telling us Roberto had been **liberated** and was being cared for in a hospital.

"How do we even know if what that telegram says is true?" Papá remarked and shook his head slowly. "We have never known for sure if he was alive or dead."

Mamá shrugged her shoulders and responded, "I don't know what to believe anymore. First he's missing, then he's dead, and now he's alive." She reached over and retied a ribbon on my dress that had come undone.

I think my parents had bravely struggled to deal with

....

captured caught and put in prison by the enemy
telegram information, notice
liberated set free

Roberto's death. They had finally **come to terms with** the loss of my brother and were now afraid that this latest information may be giving them false **expectations**. As for Roberto's sweetheart, Dolores, she had held on to hope for a while, but eventually began dating Evaristo Maldonado. I didn't blame her for going on with her life, but I guess I was just a little surprised. She and Roberto had appeared very much in love and had planned to marry as soon as he returned from the war. But Roberto's reported death had changed things for Dolores. Now things would change again. The War Department was telling us that Roberto was alive and would be coming back to us.

I picked up the telegram from the kitchen table and turned it over in my hands several times. I laid it back on the table, then picked it up again.

"What are you thinking, Nilda?" Papá asked.

"I'm thinking about Dolores. Shouldn't we tell her about this?" I asked and handed the telegram to him.

"I don't think we should say anything," Papá responded. "She's seeing Evaristo Maldonado. Better leave things alone for now."

It took weeks after the arrival of the telegram before Roberto returned home to us. He was **frail,** gaunt, and ill, but we were overjoyed to have him back in any condition. Mamá put him to

....

come to terms with accepted

expectations hope

frail weak, skinny

bed and made him chicken broth and *manzanilla* tea. She didn't want Roberto out of her sight and she hovered over him almost continuously.

My brothers, Zeke and Pete, wanted Papá to make a big fiesta, like the one we had for Roberto and Zeke when they were leaving to go to the Army.

Mamá said, "This is a great occasion for celebration, but I think we need to wait until Roberto is stronger."

But Papá celebrated. He celebrated up and down Garrapata Road with all of his *compadres* and neighbors. In fact, Mamá told my father that he should perhaps do a little work on the farm before we all starved.

The day after his return, Roberto joined me in the kitchen for a cup of coffee.

"How is Dolores? What did she say when she was told I was coming home?" he asked.

He and I were sitting across from one another at the kitchen table and Juana, our older sister, was drying dishes. Before I could respond Juana spoke up.

"Papá thought **it best not to** tell Dolores about you because she has a boyfriend. It's Evaristo Maldonado."

Roberto **stiffened** in his chair. I guess this frightened Juana,

....

compadres friends (in Spanish)
it best not to that we should not
stiffened straightened, tensed

because she dropped a cup that broke with a loud crash. Roberto gasped. Then I saw him begin to tremble. He rose to leave, but turned and smiled at Juana.

"Dolores will come back. I know she'll come back to me," he said. "She has to come back. It was only my love for her that kept me alive all the time I was a prisoner."

The news of Roberto's return traveled quickly throughout the area. A lot of friends and acquaintances from neighboring farms and ranches came by to greet Roberto and wish him well. On his third day home, Dolores and her mother arrived at our house for a visit. The meeting between Dolores and Roberto seemed to me to be rather **formal and strained**. Of course, it had been almost four years since they had seen one another. During Dolores's visit, she and Roberto walked alone out to the big *nacahuita* tree. I couldn't help but wonder what they talked about.

Later that evening when Roberto and I were alone on the screened porch, I asked, "How are things between you and Dolores?"

"A little awkward, I guess," he replied. "But I know she still loves me."

I hesitated a few seconds, then asked, "Did she say anything about Evaristo Maldonado?"

....

formal and strained uncomfortable, awkward

Roberto took a deep breath. "Not much, except she doesn't love him and she's going to tell him that she won't be seeing him anymore."

"There may be trouble. He's a real **possessive** type, *muy celoso*," I said. "I bet he won't **let go of** her very easily."

Several weeks passed and Roberto seemed to be regaining his strength. Zeke and Pete began taking him with them to Sunday afternoon baseball games. Roberto was becoming more like the brother that I had known before the war. It gave me a feeling of relief to think that things were returning to the way they had once been. I thought nothing else could happen to my family to cause so much pain and sorrow like what we had already experienced. I was wrong.

Our new problems began one night when I was awakened around midnight by the sound of a woman crying. It was coming from the screened porch where Roberto slept. I lit a lamp and went directly to the porch. There, in the light of my lantern, I saw a **disheveled** Dolores seated in a chair with Roberto standing over her. Her eyes and lips were swollen and her nose oozed blood. I noticed that her blouse was torn and her face and hands appeared to have been smeared with blood.

"My God! You've been beaten," I said as I drew closer to get

....

possessive jealous
let go of stop dating
disheveled bruised and upset

a better look.

Dolores hung her head and whimpered.

"How did this happen?" I asked.

"Be quiet. Don't wake Mamá and Papá," Roberto said.

"Did Evaristo Maldonado do this?" I asked.

"Yes," whispered Dolores. She began crying again and the blood ran faster from her nose.

"Nilda, get a basin of water and let's get her cleaned," Roberto said.

I stopped her nosebleed and washed her face and hands. The more I cleaned her, the more I realized that her clothing was wet with quite a bit of blood.

"Are you bleeding from somewhere on your body?" I asked.

Dolores shook her head.

I found it difficult to believe that a nosebleed could have soaked her in so much blood.

"Dolores, is all of this blood from your nose?" I asked.

"I don't know. Please. I just want to go home." She kept her head **bowed** and never once looked at me.

Apparently Dolores had walked to our house. Roberto said he would take her home. I stayed awake for the rest of the night in the screened porch waiting for him to return.

....

bowed down

When Roberto came home about dawn, I could tell he was ill. He quickly got into bed and began to shake. I covered him with all the blankets I could find without awakening the rest of the **household**.

"What's wrong, Roberto? Tell me," I demanded.

"I've had a fever," he replied. "And the night sweats are returning. It's a part of the sickness I've had."

Roberto was sick all day. His fever would come and go. Mamá used an entire bottle of rubbing alcohol on him to help keep his fever down.

"I guess I'll have to rub some of Nicho's whiskey on you next," Mamá said as she held up the empty alcohol bottle. "Nilda, go see if your Papá has a bottle of whiskey out in the tractor barn."

I started out the door, but stopped when I saw the sheriff's vehicle coming toward our house.

"Mamá, here comes the sheriff!"

"Well, let him come. There's nobody here but the three of us and we've done nothing wrong," she said.

The sheriff stopped in front of our house and got out of his vehicle. He started toward our house, but stopped when Mamá and I hurried out to meet him.

"Hello, Mrs. Paloma. Where's your boy, Robert?" the sheriff

....

household people in the house

asked as he **tipped his hat**.

"He's in bed very ill."

"Well. I need to talk to him. Get him out here or I'm going in," the sheriff responded.

Mamá stepped in front of the lawman.

"It's all right, Mamá," said Roberto. He was already coming out of the house.

"Have you seen Evaristo Maldonado?" the sheriff asked and pointed his finger at Roberto.

"No, I have not," Roberto quickly answered. He was **perspiring** again and his sweaty face glistened in the sun.

"Why do you ask this of my son?" Mamá said and placed her hands on her hips.

"Evaristo Maldonado is missing. I think Roberto had reason to want to hurt him."

"How do you know Evaristo is hurt?" Roberto asked.

The sheriff took a long breath and narrowed his eyes. "Because his pickup truck was found **abandoned** with blood all over the inside of the cab."

"Well, my son hasn't been out of this house in days," Mamá responded and moved closer to Roberto. "Can't you see he's sick?"

"Yes. Thank you, Mrs. Paloma. And you," the sheriff pointed

....

tipped his hat politely greeted her

perspiring sweating

abandoned empty

at Roberto again, "you don't go anywhere until I say you can."

The sheriff tipped his hat to Mamá and left.

"Quick, Nilda. Go find your Papá. And find your brothers, too."

I wasn't sure where to look. Zeke was probably off somewhere with his wife, Rita. Pete had taken Juana to the big yellow store in El Tule to buy a sack of sugar. I had no idea where Papá was. I would go see if he was at Don Tacho's, or perhaps at Don Anselmo's.

Mamá began to push Roberto toward the house. "And, Nilda, don't take the old pickup truck. Take the **flatbed**," she said.

I was gone for more than two hours looking for my father. He wasn't at the farms of our nearest neighbors. He wasn't at the big yellow store in El Tule. Pete and Juana weren't there either. I drove by Anita's Cafe and Papá's favorite *cantinas* but I could not find him. I finally gave up and went back home.

Everybody had already returned home, but Roberto was gone and so was the old pickup truck. I had barely arrived home when the sheriff showed up again.

"Why do you want to see my son, Sheriff Hunsacker?" my father asked as he opened the door for the sheriff.

The lawman stepped into our house and tipped his hat to

....

flatbed truck we use to move heavy objects

cantinas restaurants (in Spanish)

Mamá. "I need to question Roberto about the death of Evaristo Maldonado. He was found floating in a **canal** not very far from here."

"Did he drown?" I asked.

"Absolutely not. He was knifed," Sheriff Hunsacker replied.

"Well, Roberto is not here and I haven't been home all day," Papá said and shrugged his shoulders and looked toward Mamá.

The sheriff turned to my mother.

"I have no idea where he is," Mamá said as she looked the sheriff **squarely** in the face.

"I need to talk to your boy," said the sheriff. He took a few steps into the room as if to get a better look.

"Go ahead, Sheriff. Search my house. Roberto's not here," my mother said and motioned for the sheriff to go on through the house.

"No. I believe you. I'm fairly certain he's not here now."

With that the lawman turned and left. We all stood speechless looking at Mamá. She began to cry.

"He left in the old pickup truck," Mamá said.

"Do you have any idea where he went?" Papá asked.

"Yes. He'll be safe there," Mamá said as she daubed at her eyes with her apron.

....

canal waterway
squarely directly

The next few months were sad ones for our family. We were worried about Roberto. We heard nothing from him. We were also concerned about Dolores. Her family had come to our place looking for her the day after Roberto left. Her mother was frantic to find her and even had the **audacity** to tell Mamá that she didn't like the idea of her daughter running off with a murderer.

What if Roberto was a murderer? He was still my brother and I loved him. I had always been closer to him than to my other brothers. If Roberto had killed Evaristo Maldonado, it was for beating Dolores. Evaristo was known to be **a hothead**. He probably deserved to die.

Sheriff Hunsacker **hounded** us constantly. He would often stop by our house to ask us if we had heard from Roberto. He told us that he suspected Roberto had fled to Mexico, but would eventually come sneaking home. The sheriff assured us that Roberto would be caught. Sometimes the sheriff parked his vehicle down our road and watched our house as if Roberto was going to come marching down Garrapata Road in the middle of the day with the sheriff parked **in full view**.

One day, after Sheriff Hunsacker had been by our house twice in the morning, Papá announced that he and Mamá would be gone for several days.

....

audacity boldness
a hothead a violent person
hounded questioned, bothered
in full view where everyone could see him

We were eating supper when Papá said, "I have the desire to visit my old Tío Ramón. Your Mamá and I will go down to Agua Fría tomorrow." Papá smiled and added four spoonfuls of sugar to his coffee before he continued. "I want you boys to take care of the place while we're gone. And, Juana and Nilda, you take care of the boys."

"Please, Papá, may I go with you? I haven't seen Uncle Ramón since I was a little girl," I said. What I really wanted was a **little diversion**. Life had been sad for us since Roberto had gone away.

"If your Mamá *wants* you to go, then you may go," replied Papá.

Mamá didn't object. In fact, she said she had already thought of taking me along. She asked me to get some of our extra quilts ready to take. She boxed up medicines and herbs. I also saw her put some food items in the back of Papá's pickup truck. She had Pete put sleeping mats and a big container of water in the truck.

Early the next morning Mamá, Papá, and I sitting between them, crossed the Rio Grande into Mexico and headed southwest on the highway to Monterrey. After two hours, we came to the turnoff to Agua Fría. This road was unpaved and rough and in places the **ruts** were so deep that I thought that we would surely

....

little diversion change, distraction
ruts holes

have to stop. But Papá managed to keep us going.

"When I was a boy living here, we had to travel this road in a *carreta* pulled by an ox," Papá said and laughed. "But now we can go down it almost as easy in a Studebaker pickup truck."

Even though the road was terrible, I enjoyed the trip. The scenery was delightful with the mountains rising in the distance. The beauty of the land was **enchanting** and I found the **sense of isolation haunting**. We traveled for miles without seeing anything except scattered mud huts, or *jacales*, as Papá called them. We came to a fast-running river and the road ran along the river's edge. Papá found a low place where the pickup could cross the river.

After about an hour, we began seeing clusters of mud huts. When we came to the tiny village of Agua Fría, we didn't stop.

Several miles beyond the village, we turned on to a narrow road that was not much more than a path, overgrown with tall grass. The tracks were not always visible and I was afraid of becoming lost.

"Good. No one has passed through here in a while," Papá said as he **noted the overgrown condition of** the little road. "We're almost there."

Mamá must have seen Tío Ramón's *jacal* and our old pickup

....

enchanting powerful, magical
sense of isolation haunting feeling of being alone scary
noted the overgrown condition of looked down and saw
that there were no tire marks on

163

truck parked beside it before I did, because I heard her gasp and say 'Roberto' under her breath.

"Papá, how did you know Roberto was here with Tío Ramón?" I asked.

"Your mother told Roberto to come here," Papá replied.

"Now what will happen to him?" I asked.

"He'll just have to stay here. Even if the sheriff finds out where Roberto is, the Mexicans will not return him to Texas," Papá responded as he turned the truck onto the path to Tío Ramón's little farm.

Roberto was standing in the doorway of the *jacal*. I could tell by the look on his face that he was relieved to see us. Mamá began crying and hugging and kissing Roberto. Tío Ramón came out and there was a lot of handshaking, hugging, and backslapping.

I stood looking at Roberto. How sad it was I thought. My brother who was a prisoner of war for over three years, who was starved, abused, and nearly died, comes home only to **become another kind of prisoner** all because of his love for a woman. I was thinking about the irony of Roberto's situation when I saw Dolores. She had come to the doorway and was standing there looking straight into my eyes. Before I could respond, she turned

....

become another kind of prisoner be forced to live away from his family

and went back into the *jacal*.

Tío Ramón invited us into his humble home. The *jacal* was **rather primitive**, like I remembered, but it was clean and livable. Dolores had already made tortillas for supper. She offered to make more. Mamá and I prepared the rest of the evening meal and we sat around Tío Ramón's table visiting until late into the night. Dolores **hung back** and really didn't say very much. I thought she seemed nervous and a little frightened. When I found myself alone with her, I asked what she intended to do with her life.

She looked down and slowly shook her head and said, "Well, I'm sure I will stay here with Roberto."

I wondered how long she'd be able to **tolerate this desolate** life. Did she love my brother enough to live with him although he was a murderer and wanted by the authorities in Texas? Did she love him enough to share his exile?

Early the next morning we prepared to depart. While my parents were loading our things in the truck, Roberto **took me aside**.

"Please take care of Mamá," he said. "She's looking tired and old."

"I'll take care of Mamá. And you take care of yourself,

....

rather primitive not modern; old
hung back did not sit with us
tolerate this desolate stand this lonely
took me aside spoke to me in private

Roberto. I'll miss you."

"Nilda, I'm really sorry about **all of this mess**."

"Me too, Roberto. But I guess you love Dolores enough to kill for her," I said.

"No," he replied, "you're wrong. I love her enough to take the blame for her."

....

all of this mess what has happened

A Fork in the Road

Mamá saw the storm coming before I did. "Nilda, you'd better **put up the *pollitos*** before the rain gets here." She began to quickly remove the bedsheets from the clothesline.

I stopped sweeping the back porch and looked around. There were a lot of black clouds off to the southeast. It was late August and the air felt hot and muggy, just the sort of day for a bad storm or perhaps, even worse, *un chubasco*. I picked up an empty bucket and went out into the yard to gather up the chicks.

I took the noisy chicks into the washhouse and gently placed each one onto the towel I had put in the bottom of Mamá's washing machine. This was the **sanctuary** we provided our chicks when the heavy rains came. The hens could fly to the low branches of the trees, but their chicks would **perish** if not rescued.

Mamá took the sheets into the house. I stayed in the yard

....

put up the *pollitos* move the chicks
sanctuary shelter, protection
perish die

gazing down Garland Potter Road. How quickly things were changing. Many of the houses had been moved or torn down and some families had gone away. And now a **cannery** was being built about a mile from us.

A gust of wind blew a canvas chair across the yard. My eyes followed the swirling dirt out to the road and down toward the school bus stop. I was going to miss walking down the road to catch the big school bus that took us into town to school. I enjoyed being with the teachers and the other students. Now that I was finished with school I seemed to have lost some of the excitement from my life.

As I was folding the canvas chair, Chatita Chávez drove into our yard in her father's old pickup. It rattled and roared, and emitted a trail of black smoke out of its tailpipe. She got out smiling as usual and excitedly pointed toward the storm that seemed to be moving toward us.

"I can't stay long, Nilda. There's a storm coming and I need to beat it home."

I was glad to see her. "Yes, I think we're in for some bad weather. Come on in and have a cup of coffee at least," I said as I **ushered** her into our kitchen.

"I'm so excited, Nilda! You'll never guess what I just did!"

....

cannery factory
ushered showed

I stopped pouring the coffee and turned and looked at her.

"I just went over to Edinburg and registered for **junior** college," she said and looked at me and smiled. "Don't you want to go take classes with me?"

I was stunned. I didn't know what to say. How could I go to college? I didn't have any money. I gave Chatita a cup of coffee. "I don't know. I don't think I can. Isn't college expensive?"

Chatita sat down at the table and began adding sugar to her coffee. "Not really, and I'm working part-time at the packing shed on Canal Road. You could work there, too."

The wind began to gust causing the house to occasionally creak and shudder. The lightbulb hanging over the table blinked off and on and I heard a low roll of thunder in the distance.

I haltingly asked, "Do you think I could get a job at the packing shed?"

"Sure. My *primo* is the *jefe*. He'll give you a job."

Mamá came into the kitchen and **exchanged greetings with** Chatita. She must have heard our conversation.

"I think it's nice that you're going to go to college, Chatita. What will you study?" my mother asked as she joined us at the table.

"I want to be a teacher."

....

junior community
jefe boss (in Spanish)
exchanged greetings with said hello to

"*¡Una maestra! Qué bueno*," Mamá said as she patted Chatita's arm.

"A teacher?" I asked. "Don't you need **a degree**?"

"You can start teaching before you get your degree. Clarence Duncan has been teaching in Brownsville since last year and I think Zulema will start this year."

The lightbulb blinked again and went out. Mamá quickly arose from the table. "I'm going to have to bring in the lanterns. I knew I shouldn't have packed them away."

"Well, Nilda, do you want to go? Because, if you do, you can go over to Edinburg with me tomorrow."

I hesitated, then said, "Yes. I want to go." My heart was beating fast. I couldn't believe how happy I was feeling.

"But I have to talk to Mamá and Papá. What if they won't let me?"

"You can at least go with me tomorrow and find out what it's all about. I'll come by for you around eight."

Chatita left me sitting at the table staring at my cup of coffee. It seemed so unreal, this idea of me going to college. My parents had never had the opportunity for much education. Juana had quit school to get married and Roberto and Zeke had graduated from high school as I had. But college? I would be the first one in my

....

¡Una maestra! Qué bueno A teacher! That is good
(in Spanish)

a degree to graduate from a four-year college

family to go to college. Yes, college was exactly what I wanted.

The day had turned dark and the rain had started. My mother came back into the kitchen with two lanterns.

"Mamá, I need to ask you something."

She picked up a cloth and began to clean the dust from the lanterns. She looked at me and smiled.

"Mamá, if I could find a way to pay, could I take classes at the junior college?" I asked, trying to **subdue** my excitement.

She stopped cleaning and raised her eyebrows. "What would you study, *m'ija*?"

"I think I want to be a teacher," I quietly replied.

Mamá sat down at the table across from me.

"*Pues*, I would like for you to go to college," she said in a serious tone.

"What about Papá? Do you think he will allow me to go?"

"Your father wants you to be happy. If going to college and being a teacher makes you happy, then he will probably allow it," she answered.

I didn't say anything. I was enjoying the feeling of happiness and **sense of wonder that had come over me**. The two of us sat in the darkened room without speaking until I saw my mamá daubing her eyes with the hem of her apron.

----

subdue control

sense of wonder that had come over me hope that the idea of going to college had given me

"What's wrong, Mamá?"

"Nothing," she replied. "I probably got some dust in my eyes. That's all."

BEFORE YOU MOVE ON...

1. **Plot** Reread page 166. What does Nilda learn when Roberto says he loves Dolores enough "to take the blame for her"?

2. **Character's Point of View** Reread pages 171–172. How does Mamá feel about Nilda going to college?